TELL THEM EMILY SENT YOU

An Everything is Fine! Romcom

KATIE MACALISTER

Also By Katie MacAlister

Dark Ones Series
A Girl's Guide to Vampires
Sex and the Single Vampire
Sex, Lies, and Vampires
Even Vampires Get the Blues

Otherworld Dark Ones Series
Bring Out Your Dead (Novella)
The Last of the Red-Hot Vampires
The Undead in My Bed (Novella)
Fistful of Vampires Anthology
Shades of Gray (Novella)

Zorya Dark Ones Series
Zen and the Art of Vampires
Crouching Vampire, Hidden Fang
Much Ado About Vampires
Unleashed (Novella)

Goth Faire Dark Ones Series
In the Company of Vampires
Confessions of a Vampire's Girlfriend
A Tale of Two Vampires

Revelation Dark Ones Series
The Vampire Always Rises
Enthralled
Desperately Seeking Vampire

Ravenfall Dark Ones Series
Axegate Walk

Dragon Septs
Aisling Grey, Guardian Series
You Slay Me
Fire Me Up
Light My Fire
Holy Smokes
Death's Excellent Vacation
(short story)

Silver Dragon Series
Playing WIth Fire
Up In Smoke
Me and My Shadow

Light Dragon Series
Love in the Time of Dragons
The Unbearable Lightness of Dragons
Sparks Fly

Dragon Fall Series
Dragon Fall
Dragon Storm
Dragon Soul
Dragon Unbound
Dragonblight

Otherworld Adventure Series
Becoming Effrijim
Dragon Revisited

Dragon Hunter Series
Memoirs of a Dragon Huner
Day of the Dragon
A Confederacy of Dragons
You Seligh Me

Born Prophecy Series
Fireborn
Starborn
Shadowborn

Time Thief Series
Time Thief
Time Crossed (short story)
The Art of Stealing Time

Matchmaker in Wonderland Series
The Importance of Being Alice
A Midsummer Night's Romp
Daring in a Blue Dress
Perils of Paulie

Papaioannou Series
It's All Greek to Me
Ever Fallen in Love
A Tale of Two Cousins
Acropolis Now

Everything is Fine Series
Improper English
Bird of Paradise (Novella)
Men in Kilts
The Corset Diaries
A Hard Day's Knight
Blow Me Down
You Auto-Complete Me
Tell Them Emily Sent You

Noble Historical Series
Noble Intentions
Noble Destiny
The Trouble With Harry
The Truth About Leo

Paranormal Single Titles
Ain't Myth-Behaving

Mysteries
Ghost of a Chance
The Stars That We Steal From the
Night Sky

Steampunk Romance
Steamed
Company of Thieves

TELL THEM EMILY SENT YOU

OK, WHAT IS THIS?

Recently, I've discovered the joy of writing novellas and short stories that catch up with existing, much loved characters, and even sometimes dive into their murky pasts (see "Becoming Effrijim" and *Dragon Revisited* for examples).

This book, however, looks forward, not back, and updates the lives of leading characters from *Men in Kilts* (Kathie and Iain), *Blow Me Down* (Corbin and Amy), and the Emily young adult novels (Emily and Fang).

You don't need to read those books to enjoy this story, but it might give you more satisfaction to see everyone approximately sixteen years on from their respective books. Or not! You do you.

Katie Mac

ONE
GAME OF PHONES

EMILY
February 12

"Brother," I said.

"Daughter," he answered, which is probably confusing to anyone who doesn't know that everyone calls my father by the name Brother, despite (a) it not being his actual name, (b) him not being a member of a religious organization, and (c) it not being his actual name. Which I realize I said twice, but I didn't want only two pertinent points in my reference to my father. He's a three-points sort of guy.

Where was I? Oh, the call.

"Brother," I said again, and gave the side paddock a meaningful look, just as if Brother could see it. Which he couldn't, because he refuses to video chat, claiming that every time he does, his phone is screwed up for weeks after. It's not—he's just old. But I digress.

"The time has finally come," I told him, and rapped firmly on the window overlooking the aforementioned paddock. The landlady's two rescue donkeys, Elton and Elton, who lived in our paddock, were busily chomping on the new snap lock I'd put on the gate. Elton I looked ashamed, and busied himself with the empty grain bucket in apparent nonchalance, but Elton II maintained a steady, and highly discomforting, eye contact with me while he tried to consume first the metal lock, then the wooden fence itself.

"For what? Death? It comes to all of us in the end, Emily," Brother answered, *oof*ing a little as he obviously sank down into his favorite oversized leather chair. His voice had that rich timbre that it gets when he goes into one of his history lectures. "I, myself, am now well into my sixties, and I can honestly say that I stare death straight in the eye every morning when I stagger into the bathroom. There's nothing we can do to stop the relentless push, push, push of the clock as time streams past us. Take you, for instance."

"Take me where? Hey! Knock it off or I'm calling your mom, and you know how testy she gets when she has to climb the fence just to yell at you guys." I covered the mouthpiece of the phone when I bellowed the last bit, stomping as I marched out of the door, and pinned back the errant donkey with what Fang has come to call the Emily Look.

Elton I scampered off after a swift glance at my face. Elton II paused, considered what he knew about me, and wisely stopped chewing on the fence in order to casually move off. No doubt to inflict his naughtiness elsewhere, but so long as he left the fences alone, I was willing to look away for a little bit. "I swear, if Mrs. Fliss wasn't knocking a hundred quid off the monthly rent for us watching those two, I'd send them back to her farm. What? No, I have not had a hit at a crack pipe. Really, Brother! Not only do you know me better than that, but that sort of comment is seriously 1990s and not at all fitting for someone who refutes his boomerhood."

"I know that you can talk the hind leg off of one of your foster donkeys," he corrected. "And I'm not a boomer. Now, if you wouldn't mind coming to the point—not that I'm unhappy talking with you, since you only see fit to call once every few months—"

"The phone works both ways," I pointed out, giving Elton II one last gimlet glance before I checked their water and returned to the house. "It's so sad now that Sparkle and Leonardo are gone."

"I believe your mother sent a bereavement card from us both on the loss of the pony and cat. I take it you haven't gotten another? Cat, that is, since I assume you aren't looking for another rescue pony."

"No. Fang believes animals come to you when they need you, so he likes to leave us open for receiving, rather than letting me look for a couple of indoor cats."

"Ah. How is Francis?" Brother is an odd dichotomy of a man—he refuses to call Fang by anything but his given name, and yet gets highly offended when anyone calls him Henry. As he once explained to my friend Holly, he had been known as Brother since my aunt Kathie first saw him as a baby, and it just made sense to stick with the name.

As I said, Brother is a three-point sort of person, but he's still my father, and I knew he'd want to be here.

"He's delicious as ever," I said, moving back into the small cottage we rented from a neighboring farm, complete with naughty donkeys. "Handsome as the day is long, a wonderful, caring vet, and a highly talented and inventive lover."

Brother knew better than to call me out. "Good, good. All is well here, although your mother is searching for a new focus." His voice dropped even though I knew he was in his study with the door closed. "You know how she gets."

"She does love to hyperfixate on a good project," I agreed. "That actually brings me to the reason I'm calling—Fang and I have decided to get married."

"You what? One moment. CHRIS! CHRIS! COME IN HERE AND LISTEN TO YOUR DAUGHTER. SHE'S GONE INSANE. NO, THE OTHER ONE. EMILY."

I held the phone away from my ear for a few seconds until he stopped yelling. Brother put me on speakerphone just as Mom entered the room, asking, "What's all this about? I was watching a seminar on the latest Egyptian mummies discovered. Emily? Is something wrong?"

"Not a damned thing. What mummy seminar? Is it good?"

"She said she's getting married," Brother told Mom.

"Oh? That's nice. I'll email you the URL, Emily. It's put on by one of the universities. When are you and Fang having the ceremony?"

"That's what I wanted to talk to you guys about. As you know, neither of us is particularly hot and bothered about getting married—"

"If you call living in sin for fourteen years not being hot and bothered, then yes, I agree," Brother said with another *oomph* and a resulting rude noise from the leather chair as he plopped into it again. "Your sister was married at twenty."

"I am not Bess. Fang is not Monk. We are stable people with jobs and responsibilities," I pointed out, not wanting to dis my sister. She had always been one to follow her own path, and if she spent the last fifteen years deep into animal rights, that was her business. "Fang and I looked at the calendar, and there are three dates that work with our schedules." I gave them the date options for the next six months.

"August?" Brother's voice rose half an octave. "You did say August, didn't you?"

"August eighteenth, yes. That's a Saturday, so we planned to take Friday and Monday off for the festivities. We won't be having a real honeymoon, but there's a small hotel in Cornwall that we absolutely love, and they said they could do a micro wedding for us, and that we would have the run of the hotel, because there are only eight rooms. We can stay on through Monday and we're happy to spend the extra time with you guys, because we can honeymoon anytime."

Mom asked questions about the small hotel that perched on a chalky cliff overlooking the sea. It was our favorite getaway place, and I knew my family would love it, as well.

The whole time we were discussing the hotel, and what family could make it to England—keeping in mind we had to limit participation to ten to twelve people—the sounds of fingers tapping on a keyboard were audible. I was about to ask Brother why he was not interested in the wedding when he interrupted Mom musing about whether they could tack on a week to have a vacation in England.

"I knew it!" Brother crowed. "And you think my memory is going, Chris! Well, this is proof it's as sound as ever."

"What is?" Mom asked.

"The International Medievalist Educators' Society Annual Mystery Tour."

"The what, now?" I asked.

"It's a weeklong mystery tour and contest organized by a group of my colleagues," Brother answered, sounding more like a hyper twelve-year-old at Comic Con than a middle-aged medieval-history professor. "I've always wanted to go on it, but we were never in England at the right time. Well, your wedding is smack-dab in the middle of the tour. I'll be able to go on it after all! Don Setlo—you remember him, Chris; he left Stanford to go to that new university that started in Belgium—Don was telling me that last year's tour had them going behind the scenes of the *Mousetrap* play in London, and they got to meet the cast, as well as tour Agatha Christie's house later." Brother's words seemed to tumble over one another, his voice rising with excitement.

Mom was made of much more phlegmatic stuff. "It does seem like the timing is right for a visit, but,

Brother, you won't want to miss walking Emily down the aisle."

"That's all right," I said quickly, not wanting to build expectations that I preferred remain out of sight.

"Emily doesn't want me hanging around for days before the wedding," Brother protested. "Do you, Emily? No, of course she doesn't. Besides, it's not as if you'll never see me. The tour leaves several hours out of each day for personal time. I can pop over to where you are whenever I want."

"Brother—" Mom started to say.

"That sounds good to me," I interrupted, flipping on the electric kettle. "I don't mind Brother having his tour around the wedding. It's only for a week, and if you guys are here for the week or so after, then we'll have loads of time together."

"But the wedding—" Mom tried again to protest. "It's your wedding, Emily. I wouldn't want you making a rash choice you'll regret just to please your father."

"Eh," I said, fishing out a bag of my favorite orange spice tea from Seattle. Brother sputtered in the background about knowing me better than Mom, and that he was certain I was down with the tour. "We're not really doing any pre-events other than the stag and hen parties. I imagine Fang would survive if Brother didn't go to the stag party. And if he can pop over to the hotel during downtime, then that's fine with me. Neither Fang nor I particularly cares about the ceremony except for legal reasons, so it's going to be very low-key—"

"Legal reasons? *Deus rex!* You're not pregnant, are you?" Brother asked, his voice now flinty with suspicion.

I fought the urge to giggle. Brother informed Bess and me every year that he was not yet ready to become a grandfather, and if we could both keep our ovaries on lockdown, he'd tell us when the time was right for us to fire off kids.

"No. I told you Fang got snipped a few years ago, and just as soon as my doctor admits I'm old enough at thirty-two to decide whether or not I want kids, I'll have my tubes tied to be doubly sure. We're animal people, not kid people."

"A wise choice," Mom murmured. "Not that I regret having you or your sister, but if we'd settled down with cocker spaniels instead of thinking we could raise intellectual children who would better the world, life would have been a great deal easier. It looks like we could add twelve days to the trip before your classes start, Brother."

He snorted something in Latin, then tapped more on the keyboard.

"So you two are a go, then," I said fifteen minutes later, after Mom and I chatted about the plans, and Brother and I convinced her that I would not be secretly heartbroken to not have my parents at my side every minute of the day.

"Yes," she said slowly, in the same dreamy voice she got when she was considering her Next Big Thing. "You know, one of the ladies in my book club mentioned that her cousin in Scotland has started a school for Neo-Picts, teaching ancient fiber arts and the like. They have woad dyeing. I've always been passionate about woad."

"Odd, but true," I said, wondering if I should take the last of the cookies that Fang and I favored, then decided that the love of my life deserved them after having to get up at four a.m.

"If you truly don't mind us not being in attendance before your wedding …" Mom let the sentence dribble to an end.

"I absolutely do not mind. I've got a project deadline two days before you'd arrive, and I'm going to be dead tired from dealing with the idiot team who refuses to listen to reason. You go indulge in the wild Pictish woad without a worry about us," I answered with perfect honesty.

Brother signed up for his mystery tour with a lot of exclamations and declarations that "This year, the Brits are going to have to contend with a strong American contingent," then asked, "What are you yammering about?"

"Let me know if you get any of those logic puzzles that have you filling in grids. I love doing those. Fang is good on the crosswords. And I was not yammering. I said that Aunt Kathie is next on my list to call. Er … should I ask Grandma?"

"Hmm," Mom said, obviously thinking about it. "Brother, what do you think?"

The keyboard clacked away wildly. "I think that I'm going to have to buy a couple of British crossword books in case Francis isn't handy. The tour committee is sure to throw crosswords in as one of the daily puzzles to solve, and I—no!"

"No, what?" I asked, yawning. Fang had been called out in the middle of the night for a bovine-related emergency, and I'd ended up staying awake after he left, running through the endless list of things I needed to get done.

"No as in I don't believe it." Brother spoke in a hushed tone, as if he were in one of his beloved cathedrals. "This year's author is Sir Arthur Conan Doyle, and the tour organizers say they're waiting for final approval to set up not only a visit to Conan Doyle's home, but a tea with one of his living relatives. His actual relative!"

"Wow," I said, seriously impressed. "That is very cool."

Like Brother, I had a deep and abiding love of mysteries, and also shared a passion for those books written in the first thirty years of the twentieth century. I'd grown up cutting my literary teeth on Conan Doyle, Agatha Christie, and Dorothy L. Sayers, so I understood just how thrilling was the thought of visiting Sir Arthur's home and having tea with one of his relations.

I gave in to temptation. "Can you take a visitor with you, Brother? Just for the visit and tea? I'd pay my own way if you could."

"I'll ask," he answered, followed by more key clicks. "I'm going to sign up now in case they get a sudden rush of participants, and we'll work out the logistics later."

"Grandma?" I prompted my mother.

"I don't think so, dear," she answered, sounding distant as if she'd moved away from Brother's phone and was looking through a Neo-Pict course catalog. "She's getting close to ninety, and that many hours in a plane wouldn't be good for her legs. What about Dru?"

"She's going to try, but she just found out she's pregnant again, and she'll be about eight months by wedding time. Don't mention it to anyone, please. She says they're going to wait to announce it, although both their parents know. Holly and her wife, Marla, are coming, though."

"You'll ask your sister, of course," Mom said a few minutes later, when I had finished my tea and was seriously reconsidering eating the last two cookies.

"I've left a message for her to call me, although god knows why she's using a vegan bakery as her answering service. In fact, they didn't want to take the message until I told them I was Bess's sister, and then all they said was that she was on the continent working with a group to take down a fur-processing plant. You know that I admire what Bess and Monk are doing, but damn. They live like they're eco–Jason Bournes."

Mom murmured something in an increasingly distracted tone, so I said my goodbyes, and flopped down on the couch, suddenly hit with a sense of grief, loneliness, and isolation.

That's how Fang found me an hour and a quarter later.

"How did the calls go—ah, Emily. Not another Leonardo day?"

I lay curled up in a ball on the couch, clutching a small blue scrap of blanket.

He pulled me upright, sat down in my spot, then opened his arms. I splatted myself against his chest, trying hard not to cry on him, but he was so warm, and solid, and wonderful, that even though he stank of a particularly slovenly barnyard, just holding him made life infinitely better. "I know. It's pathetic of me to still be crying over a cat who lived his life the way he wanted, and died surrounded with his family, but it just kind of hit me after I got off the phone with Mom and Brother."

"I told you that we can get another cat," Fang said into my hair, rubbing my back as I snuggled into him, relishing his body heat. "We can go to the animal society this afternoon and pick one out."

"No," I said, leaning far to the side to blow my nose before returning to droop on him. "It's your turn. We agreed that the next pet would be a dog."

"But you're sad because Leonardo is gone," he pointed out in that matter-of-fact manner that sometimes irritated me, but mostly made me grateful he counteracted my impulsiveness so nicely. "And since you're working from home, it makes sense for you to have a cat as a daytime companion. Speaking of which—" He glanced at the clock. "I only have twenty minutes, and I need to change before I go in to the office for the afternoon appointments."

"We'll get a dog," I told him fifteen minutes later when he'd had a fast shower and changed to clean clothes more suited to a handsome—if taken—vet in a thriving Cotswolds practice. "I like dogs, Fang. You know this. If we get a dog, he can be my buddy, and I'll stop having blue Leonardo days."

He paused on his way out the door and tipped my head back, his lovely peaty-brown eyes smiling at me as he said against my lips, "I love you beyond reason. You know this, yes?"

"Yes," I said, biting his lower lip until he kissed me the way I wanted. "Because I'm just as unreasonable about you."

"We'll get both a dog and a cat," he said, kissed me soundly, and squeezed my left butt cheek before hurrying off.

"Sexy, loving, and with exceptionally good brains," I said, waving as he tooted the car horn at me when he drove off with a cloud of warm exhaust on the cold air. I clutched Leonardo's blue blanket, and told it, "If he isn't the perfect man, then I don't know who is. And he's mine, mine, mine. A cat *and* a dog. Hmm. Let's think about this, shall we?"

Thankfully, the blanket didn't answer. I did keep it with me for the rest of the day, but my spirits felt a bit brighter, as if Leonardo approved of the plan.

TWO
THE G.O.A.T. GOAT

KATHIE
13 February

"Benedict Bandersnatch is a jerk!"

I looked up from my laptop to eye the flushed face glaring into my office. "I fervently hope you are talking about your goat, and not the actor of a similar name, because he is awesome, and your goat is not."

Clara gasped the gasp of a fourteen-year-old goatherd who assigned human personalities to every single one of her beloved twelve goats. "Mum! How can you say that? My goats are the GOAT. No other goats give as much milk as they do. Plus they're smart and clean, and Dad says that they are the best-smelling goats he's ever seen. Their TikTok game is strong. And they've won awards!"

"You're right, I'm wrong, and you can please nip in the bud the lecture I can see you badly want to give me. Tell me, how do you feel about being a bridesmaid?"

The second love of my life—the first being my delectable husband, Iain—gave me a look initially sour, but which morphed after a few seconds into one of speculation. "Are you and Dad getting married again? Can I officiate? You said that our membership into the Church of the Flying Spaghetti Monster means I can marry people. I'll wear a kilt to do it. Is Grandma coming for the wedding? She promised to bring me the outfits she kept from when she was young. I could do all sorts of shots of the goats with me in flower-power dresses. Maybe I should make a new soap for the wedding? People love special-event soaps."

I had to wait until she paused to take a breath before I could answer. "Dad and I are not going to have another ceremony—one was enough, thank you, although your father's side of the family looked stunning in all their kilted glory." I spent a few minutes gazing at our wedding picture, which I had cropped down to just Iain standing outside a ruined Scottish castle in full kilt. Although he had more threads of gray in his hair now, he was still just as gorgeous as when I'd met him some fifteen years earlier. "Emily is going to finally marry Fang, and she said she'd be happy to have you be a bridesmaid if you want."

"Oh." Clara leaned against the doorframe, and pursed her lips. "I suppose that would be OK. Would I have to wear some horrible poufy dress?"

I was well aware that Clara was going through a bit of a clothing-conscious stage, where the selection and wearing of certain garments became of tantamount importance to her. "I doubt it. For one, Emily is not a poufy-dress sort of person. In fact, I'm willing to bet she'll show up in a very nontraditional dress, if she even wears one."

There was more lip pursing from Clara before she straightened up. "OK."

"It'll be during the week you're off, so there shouldn't be a conflict there, although I'm hoping we'll be able to stay in Cornwall for a couple of days as a holiday."

"I don't know that I can do that," Clara said with a shake of her head. "I have responsibilities, you know. August is the summer beach-party promotion, so I'll have to be here watching everything. But I can take a day off for Emily." A shadow loomed over Clara, who glanced over her shoulder. "Also, August is the time when I pick out the bucks for the girls. I want to do maternity shots this year. Someone did them on IG last year, and she got a ton of response. Are you going to Emily's wedding, Uncle Ewan?"

"I have no knowledge of this event, but if you mean your cousin, then I would be delighted should I be invited, although I could have sworn she married her vet some time ago." Ewan, Iain's older brother, who looked and sounded like he'd stepped straight off a plummy BBC show, moved into sight and cocked an eyebrow at me.

"I'll ask Emily, but she mentioned keeping the numbers down, due to a small facility," I told him.

"I'm going to the soap barn. I want to try running another batch of frankincense, since the last one was a hideous failure because Lara put in way more oil than I told her. Honestly, Mum, it's like she does it on purpose! When I pointed out that her batch turned out a mess, her face went all red and scrunched, and she cried and went home, and Joanna said she was trying, but everyone makes mistakes. I'm fine with mistakes! I just don't want my name on soap that disintegrates the second it gets wet because *someone* put in too much frankincense. It's common sense, after all." Clara marched off without allowing me to respond.

"That girl gets more and more like Iain every day," Ewan commented, looking after her. "The word phlegmatic comes to mind, but I suppose that's a bit harsh considering she's, what, twelve?"

"Fourteen going on forty," I said with one of the martyred sighs that both Iain and I had become experts at over the last ten years or so. "And yes, she's very like him. The farm is in her blood just like it's in his."

"There's a fair bit of you in her, as well," Ewan said with a flash of his devastating smile, the one that had garnered him six wives over the course of his lifetime. "She's very enterprising, and that's something about which the little man never cared."

"I don't agree at all—Iain is very entrepreneurial. He has to be, running a sheep farm of this size. Although thankfully now that David has taken over half the land, it'll soon be less stressful. Once we get David through his first year, anyway. Do you really want to go to Emily's wedding?"

He thought for a moment, then sighed. "I wouldn't mind—I always enjoy seeing your family, since they are refreshingly unique—but Zoe would no doubt have something to say about it. Where is it to be held?"

I glanced at the note I'd scribbled during my brief call with Emily, and read him the name and address of the hotel. "It's in Cornwall, and evidently quite charming and quaint. What are the odds I can get Iain into a kilt for it, do you think?"

"None I would take," Ewan said with a shake of his head, pulling out his phone when it chirped at him. He answered, saying, "I'm here, my sweet one, ready to worship at your feet," as he moved off through the door out to the small garden where I banned all animals in an attempt to grow a few vegetables. "Yes, yes, I will leave here shortly to return to your side. ..."

I made a mental note to tell Iain that Ewan was evidently still on good terms with wife number six, and idly wondered why she reminded me of Lilith from the *Frasier* TV show. "Maybe it's the deadpan delivery," I murmured to myself as I got up, fetched my pair of sunflower-covered wellies, and, tucking the sticky note with the date of the wedding into my pocket, headed out toward the stable. "That or the way she wears her hair, and bites the end off of words. Hello, Sunshine. Shall we go out for a bit? Damsel, wake up."

This time of year, we put the horses into a pasture that ran the length of the drive out to the road, giving passersby a lovely pastoral view of horses grazing peacefully, while behind them rose the cozy barn we built the year before, and beyond that, the small white farmhouse, which also sported a new addition in the form of a soap workshop. I spoke loudly as I made my way toward the sunny patch of the pasture, which just happened to be next to the road.

As I called to Sunshine, the blind rescue we'd taken in with her companion, Damselfly, I saw a car slow down, no doubt impressed by the scenic image of a pure white mare grazing peacefully next to a gangly and very tall chestnut gelding.

Only the gelding in question was laying his lazy self down in the sunny patch, which, if you did not know just how lazy he was, and how he loved nothing more than to take naps, you might mistake for a horse in trouble.

"How dare you!"

The voice that broke the tranquil, if chilly, February air was feminine and, as I approached the horses, appeared to be coming from the car.

"Eh?" I said, confused. "Sunshine, it's just me coming up on your left. No, that's not a snake, it's the halter. The very same halter you've smelled every day for the last six years. Lady, what is it you want? You're scaring my horse. She's blind, and she doesn't like loud noises, so if you could turn down your volume a couple of notches, I'd be grateful."

"How dare you!" she said for the fifth time, having repeated herself while I was warning Sunshine of my location, although she did stop screaming it. Most likely that was because I led Sunshine a few steps toward the fence, so I could converse in a more polite volume.

"How dare I have a blind horse? Or how dare I ride her? The vet was adamant that as long as she's comfortable, and I'm taking care of where we go, then the exercise and mental stimulation is good for her."

"How dare you leave that!" the woman said, sticking one hand out the open window to wave at Damsel.

I looked over at him. "He's her companion horse. They're a bonded pair. It would be cruel not to take him in, as well."

"He's dead!" The woman was back to screeching again. She clutched the car door as she leaned out the window. "You have a dead horse right there where anyone can see it! My children have seen it! They have seen a dead horse! They are traumatized! What is wrong with you Scotmens that you leave dead animals lying around to traumatize innocent children?"

The writer in me was not able to let some things pass. "Scotsmen, I believe, is the correct—"

"I have half a mind to film you and your atrocious animal husbandry, and put it online for everyone to see!"

"She admitted she has half a mind," I told Sunshine. "You heard it. I don't have to say it, do I?"

Sunshine, who was groaning slightly as I scratched a particularly favorite spot behind one ear, flipped her head a couple of times.

"I'm so glad you agree. Damsel, get up. No, you are not dead, no matter how still you try to be. Dead horses don't have the oomph to flip their tails around, and yours hasn't stopped the whole time those people over there have been confused about you. Lady, for the love of god, stop! I told you he's a rescue horse. He lives for drama, but he's also Sunshine's bestie. See? He's fine."

Damsel, never one to turn down a chance at the grain bucket, picked up his head to look at me when I shook the bucket as I spoke. With a prodigious fart, he got to his feet, shook himself, then, with sublime indifference to the woman who was still hanging out of the window lambasting me, wandered over and stuck his face into the bucket.

Whoever was at the wheel of the car drove off while the woman was in the middle of another rant, which just made me laugh all the way back to the barn. I got Sunshine saddled, and with Damsel tethered to me so Sunshine knew he was there, we headed out at a brisk walk to find the man who still made my pulse quicken.

I knew the minute I saw Iain that something was wrong.

He stood next to one of the two quad bikes that he and Mark—our shepherd, and one of Iain's oldest friends—used to get around the hills. Although Iain stood with his back to me, silhouetted against the pale winter sun, the drooped set of his shoulders told me all was not well.

"Just a warning, Sunshine: I'm going to speak loudly in five seconds, so don't be startled when I suddenly yell. WHAT'S WRONG?" I more or less bellowed the last two words.

Iain turned as I rode up, making me gasp and pull up sharper than I intended. Sunshine—who used a bitless bridle—snorted and shook her head at my poor horsemanship, but happily took two steps forward in order to snuffle Iain for signs of potential treats.

"What the hell?" I asked, slowly dismounting and tying Sunshine's reins to the quad. "Iain, why is your beautiful face bloody and swollen, and is that a black eye?" I stood in front of him, wanting to reach out and wipe away the blood and dirt, but unable to do so because he looked so miserable.

"I went and fell off the bluidy mountain, didn't I?" he answered, patting his pockets.

I wanted to laugh at the statement, since it's one I had said the day I arrived at the farm. "You fell on your face? No, sit, and let me get some of the mud off." I pulled out the handful of tissues and sanitizer wipes, and waited for him to gingerly sit on the running board. "Did you hurt anything else? You're kind of listing to one side."

He hesitated for a dozen seconds, swearing in Gaelic under his breath as I dabbed at his gory face. "Aye, I'm a right bourach. My ribs are a bit bruised, and I think my knee's blown out. I can't bear much weight on it."

"Gotcha," I said, trying hard to calm the urge to stand up and scream for someone to help. Over the years, I've managed to soak up some of Iain's calm, which I was grateful for at that moment. I certainly wouldn't have been standing around silently if I was as hurt as he was, that's for sure. "Where's Mark?"

"He's over toward Leery's lifting the BFL ewes. No, love, don't bother—I already called him and told him to keep moving the sheep. We need them out of there while Leery puts up the new fence. Just give me a minute to get myself sorted—then I'll finish up with the cheviot ewes."

"Not if you can't walk, you won't. Can you drive?" I tried to assess just how hurt he was, and whether I needed to call for medical aid. Iain came from seriously stoic ancestors (Vikings, no doubt, interbred with wild Celts), so it was always difficult to gauge the seriousness of any injury or illness.

"Aye, but I'm not going to use the bike to lift the ewes." Iain frowned while I continued to wipe blood and muck from his face. "I'll be fine in a few minutes. Or fine enough to finish up, then I'll go back and put something cold on my knee."

"Oh, you'll be doing a lot more than putting frozen peas on your knee," I told him, tapping on my phone. "Ewan! Have you left yet?"

"An hour ago, my lovely one," came his reply.

"Damn. Never mind. David is closer." I promised Ewan an explanation later, and rang Iain's youngest son (and our next-door neighbor, separated only by forty or so acres of hill and pasture). "David! I don't suppose you are anywhere near your dad's side of the farm? No? Well, how soon can you get here?"

"Kathie, I just said I'd take care of this," Iain said sternly, and tried to grab my phone. I didn't miss the spasm of pain that followed him reaching for it, so I moved backward a couple of steps, which allowed Sunshine—who had been bopping me on the back with her velvety nose—to shift forward, and resume checking out Iain.

"Is something wrong?" David asked, sounding a bit out of breath.

"Yes, but I don't think it's lethal. Iain fell and smashed his face, and his ribs and knee are bad. He's got the quad, but there's no way he can shift the herd up here."

"Flock," David said in my ear at the same time Iain said the same word, shooting me a look that mingled love, annoyance, and, in the end, resignation.

"Do you need help moving him?" David's breathing increased as if he was running. "I'll head your way now, but I'm in the south. Should I ring 999?"

"Hang on, your father is going to explode if I don't let him talk," I told David, then handed Iain my phone. I made a mental note about lecturing him later about the folly of not calling me to tell me he'd injured himself, and eyed first the quad, then Damsel.

It took two minutes of arguing from both David and me before Iain agreed to take himself back to the house, so we could assess the state of his injuries.

"Would it be easier for you to ride instead of drive?" I asked him as I helped him to his feet. He grunted and swore, grabbing for the seat to steady himself. "Oh, lord, Iain. You can't drive this way. Let me see. If it was Damsel by himself, I'd leave him in the pasture, but Sunshine—"

"It's all right, love. I can drive. I just need to get in," he said.

I really don't want to think about the four minutes that followed. Iain's knee had swollen up and refused to bend to the point where he—a tall man—could stuff it into the footwell. We managed to get him relatively comfortable, but I could tell it cost him a lot.

"Drive slowly. I don't want to think of what you'd look like if you rolled the quad," I told him when he, with his best sheepdog, Mabel, at his side, turned and headed down the hill.

By the time I got the horses back to their pasture (and promised them a brushing later), Iain was ensconced on the couch, covered in a down blanket, with his daughter-in-law Joanna puttering around.

"Oooh, thank you. It's colder than I thought it would be up on the hills," I told her when she handed me a cup of tea. I took a couple of sips of it to warm up, then lifted the edge of Iain's blanket. "Holy shit!"

"David's coming as soon as he moves the sheep," Joanna said, bringing me an ice pack wrapped in a towel. She averted her eyes as she did so, but I said nothing. She had three boys ranging between fifteen and eight, but she was squeamish to the point of passing out if an injury was too gruesome. "He'll help get Dad into the car."

"Could you get into my car if I helped you?" I asked Iain, studying the mess that was his knee. I suspected the kneecap was dislocated, but there was definitely some internal injury, since it was bruising a prodigious plum color. I got the ice pack settled before covering his legs again. "It's lower to the ground and would be easier to get into."

"I can't bend my leg," he said in an apologetic tone. "I'll be fine here. The ice'll help my knee."

"Nothing is going to help that but medical aid. Right. I'm not going to wait for David. We're going to get you into the car. Joanna?"

"I'll do whatever I can," she said, ignoring the baleful look Iain turned on her.

It took a further seven minutes before I put down the back seats of my car, made Iain a nest of blankets and pillows, and, with Joanna's help propping him up, got him into the back of my car.

"What's Dad doing?" Clara asked when she emerged from her soap workshop. She was flushed, and smelled of a complex mix of pine, cedar, and citrus. "Why is he in the back? Are you going into town? I need to go to the co-op to pick up some supplies. Can I get a ride?"

"I'll run you into town quickly, Clara," Joanna offered. "Your parents are a bit busy right now."

"I'm fine, love. Just a bad knee," Iain told her, wincing as he made himself comfortable. He was pressed with his back against the passenger front seat, his long legs angled to fit. "You know how your mum is."

"Sane?" I asked as I got into the driver's seat. "Smart? Well aware of how stupidly high your pain threshold is?"

"Worried," Iain said, but his lips twitched a few times.

"I'll take you into town later, Clara, or you can go with Joanna if she doesn't mind hauling your things."

Joanna, who was now on the phone telling her youngest son that she could see he was playing on the Xbox and not cleaning the chicken coop as he should be doing, nodded quickly at Clara and gestured toward her car.

Six hours, forty-four minutes, and a handful of seconds later, we arrived home, and, with Clara and David's help, got Iain inside and comfortable on the daybed in the lounge.

"So," David said, moving over to where a few bottles and glasses sat on a beautiful antique kitchen dresser. Iain had nodded meaningfully at the bottles, a fact I ignored as I consulted the information provided with Iain's four prescriptions. "I looked up the long Latin terms you sent me, Dad, and other than some extremely gruesome pictures, I reckon it's a broken knee?"

"Aye, a bit." Iain frowned when I took the glass David brought, drank half of it, and let Iain have the remainder.

"Don't give me that look," I told him. "You had opioids four hours ago. I'm sure even the quarter cup of whiskey that's left is not something you should have on top of them, but since you have two hours until your next pain meds, I'm prepared to risk it. Clara, would you turn the kettle on? David, you are beyond worth your weight in gold for all the help. Clara and I can handle it from here, so go home to your family."

"Whiskey is far better for me than pain medications," Iain groused, but the outer edges of his eyelids drooped, and his body language told me he wasn't feeling quite so perky as he'd like everyone to believe. "I don't need to become addicted to painkillers just because a few bones in my knee failed me."

"And the three ribs," I said, adjusting a couple of pillows behind him, and dragging over a kitchen chair for visitors, and a half-moon table from the hall to hold the tea that Clara was making, his phone, the TV remote, and sundry other things that I knew he'd need for the next few days he'd have to stay off his feet. "And let's not forget that crack on your collarbone."

"It was two ribs, not three," Iain argued, allowing me to layer a couple of throws next to him, ready for him to use as needed. "And that doctor who looked younger than Clara said he wasn't sure about the crack. It was barely there if it was at all."

I ignored the dubious nature of the crack in his collarbone. "Of course, no one can forget about the—not one, but two—black eyes courtesy of the rock you smashed your face into. You're just lucky you didn't break your nose. Oh, Iain." I sat down on the chair, not wanting to jiggle the daybed mattress. "I love you until the end of time, but man alive, you look like someone tied you to Damsel, hauled you through the hedge backward, then turned around and repeated that three more times."

He started to laugh, yelped, and wrapped his arms around himself.

"Sorry. I swear I won't be funny," I promised, instantly feeling guilty for causing him pain. I wanted to hover around him and do something, anything, to make him feel better, but Iain, as I have had cause to note for many years, was the personification of the word stoic. He disliked hovering solicitude, so after checking that he'd be OK, I went off to deal with dinner for all the animals.

"Did you think more about whether you want to be Emily's bridesmaid?" I asked when Clara and I hustled the chickens into their coop, and fed the goats, horses, barn cats, as well as six elderly ewes that we had convinced Iain had too much character to be anything but our pets, and which, when let out from their paddock, tended to follow Clara and me with a level of slavish devotion that led me to believe they knew how luck had favored them. "You don't have to do it—Emily will understand if you feel like it's not your jam."

"Vibe, Mum. People vibe, they don't jam. And I don't care either way about being a bridesmaid. I suppose it would be OK. How bad is Dad hurt?"

Ah, so that's why she was so quiet. As a rule, Clara took after her father … except when it came to communication.

She got her verbosity and empathy from me, leaving her prone to chattering nonstop.

"He will likely have to have surgery on that knee as soon as the swelling goes down," I said slowly, our shadows long, inky blobs from the yard lights. The air was still, but cold, and as I glanced up, I couldn't help but notice some clouds rolling in from the east. I had a feeling a storm was coming … and not just one confined to weather. "The ribs will mend quick enough, the doctor said. So long as your father doesn't try to do things."

Clara, who had a wheelbarrow full of muck on her way to the compost pit, paused to give me a look.

"Yeah, he doesn't know Iain at all. But you and I together ought to keep him from doing too much too fast."

She made a face and trundled past the storage shed, saying as she passed, "You'll be able to stop him. He'll do anything to make you happy. I mean, Bathsheepa."

I glanced back at the paddock with the sheep, now happily gathered around the hay we'd given them as part of their winter feed. Bathsheepa IV was an elderly sheep with the cutest black muzzle and only one ear, who, when she was feeling particularly joyous, was known to run full tilt into my knees.

Ever since the first little lamb I'd named Bathsheepa had died, Iain turned a blind eye to me picking one less-than-thriving lamb each season, and raising it as a pet. He didn't outright approve, but over the years, he realized just how much it meant to me—and now Clara—and didn't even kick up a fuss when our pet flock grew.

I returned to the house, and immediately went to the doorway of the sitting room to see if Iain had fallen asleep, as I had hoped.

His head turned as I leaned against the doorframe. "Ah, love. I've made a right muck of things this time."

"No, you haven't." I knelt on the floor next to the daybed, holding his hand and rubbing his knuckles on my cheek. I loved Iain's hands. They were large, but with long, sensitive fingers, like the fingers of a violinist. They were also crisscrossed with myriad scars, but they were the hands of a man who could ease a breech-birth lamb into the world with the same gentleness as when he touched me. "But this sign, I think, is one we can't ignore."

He closed his eyes, but I saw the flash of pain in them. "Aye. I know. But I'm not ready to leave the farm yet. David's not up to speed, even if I was. If I kept to the lowlands ... if I hired another hand—"

"I want you to make a deal with me," I interrupted, and, checking the time, handed him his pain medication. "You don't lay here and worry about the future, and I'll agree to us staying here until you're absolutely one hundred and ten percent sure you want to leave. Deal?"

He smiled, but there were pain lines alongside his mouth, and his eyes looked a bit bleary. "I'll take that deal. So long as I have you and the weans, I'll be happy."

"Mm-hmm. Take a nap, and don't fash yerself," I said in my best Scottish accent.

The fact that he didn't argue told me a lot, and I set about fixing dinner with increased concern.

Iain was a very fit man, to the point where his doctor claimed he could pass for a good ten years younger, but even he couldn't be expected to climb hills and ramble up and down sides of mountains for decades without it starting to take a toll on his body.

"And I like his body far too much to let it be harmed," I muttered to myself as I flung stew into the oven to warm while I whipped up some corn bread. "Either the farm has to change or we do, and I'm sure as hell not going to break Iain's heart by asking him to become someone else. We're simply going to have to reevaluate the farm. The solution has to be here."

Brave words, gentle reader. Not particularly prescient ones, but still … brave.

THREE
HIPS DON'T LIE

AMY
August 10

"Corbin, why is there an anatomically correct naked half-elf wizard dancing on top of the inn mailbox?" I paused on the way out of the bathroom and cocked an eyebrow at the man who lounged on the bed with four pillows stuffed behind him, and a laptop on his legs. "My mother always warned the day would come when you would cast your eyes asunder, but I never thought it would be at a naked wizard."

"Look, I can't help the fact that I'm such a good artist that I can turn on even happily married men with my naked male dancing wizards," came a voice from the laptop, and I noticed a small square in the upper corner with a familiar face. I tugged up the top edge of the bath towel wrapped around my torso. Since it was big enough to cover me from collarbone to knees, I simply waved before moving out of the camera's view. "Not that I condone such a thing, especially when I was the one who married you two together into the bonds of piratical matrimony, but far be it from me to ignore the elephant in the room, and that elephant is I'm too good for the likes of you."

"Uh-huh," I told Holder MacReady, Corbin's oldest friend, and the head of art for Buckling Swashes. "I only married him because he said you were threatening to force him into matrimony with a sheep. Why is there a fully nude elf? I thought you guys decided to disable the nudity option?"

"We did," Corbin said, waggling his eyebrows at me when I slid onto the bed next to him. "But there's a graphics glitch that Holder is trying to pinpoint. Whenever characters log off and back in while they are at an inn, their armor disappears. It's something to do with the code checking the database to see what armor each player has acquired."

He put a hand on my bare thigh as he spoke, his fingers stroking my leg in a manner that had me looking sideways at him. We'd had a lovely romp in the sheets during the middle of the night—we were still getting used to being in London rather than back home in California—but that didn't mean we couldn't indulge ourselves again.

"It's more than just a glitch at this point," Holder said, his voice filled with disgust. He turned to look at another monitor and started reading out a list of highly technical issues that I—the sole programming Luddite in a family filled with computer geniuses—decided wasn't at all conducive to romance.

Corbin and Holder discussed the issues while I leaned back against the headboard and took a minute to consider my life, an occurrence that became more common as we slowly drifted into middle age.

"I think it goes beyond the database, Corb," Holder said as he typed madly, then paused to squint at the monitor again. "It's almost as if it's the AI itself that is removing the armor."

"That's not within its purview," Corbin said, shaking his head.

I studied his profile, musing over the fact that although we'd been married for over ten years, just the sight of him made me feel like butterflies were careening off the inside of my stomach. "Why isn't it possible? You told me AI is growing by exponential leaps and bounds. What if it's thinking for itself, and for some reason, it feels like it has to gather up people's armor?"

"Our AI doesn't do that," Corbin said at the same time Holder shook his head and told me, "It's limited to powering the NPCs and mobs. It can't do anything on its own that we don't first program into it."

I leaned to the side so I could pin Holder back with a steely gaze.

He had the grace to grin. "OK," he admitted. "There is the remote—and I mean seriously remote—idea that someone could pull a Paul on us, and corrupt the code without us knowing, but ever since we painstakingly rewrote all the code for Buckling Swashes, we eliminated any opportunity of a repeat situation. No one is going to get locked into *Placeholder*. Corbin made sure of that."

"Much though I think back on our time stuck in the game with a fine appreciation of how well the virtual reality part worked, I figured we didn't need a repeat of that, and put in three different safeguards to keep it from happening again," Corbin told me, glancing at me when I trailed a finger down his naked back.

I smiled. He sat up straight, his eyes alight with interest.

"The truth is, I think we need to bring in Ash." Holder made a disgusted sound and spun around in his chair to tap at a different computer's keyboard.

Corbin's attention was immediately averted. "Asher as in your wife's nephew? Why? He's not an expert in graphics or the programming suite we use. Isn't he with the NSA or something?"

"That was just an unfortunate phase he went through," Holder said, waving away the idea. "He's with a highly secret white hat organization now, working on how AI can be used for security vulnerabilities."

"You both just got done saying that whatever the issue is with the naked half-elf, it couldn't be AI," I pointed out, drawn into the conversation despite my sudden need to frolic all over Corbin's delectable self. Our anniversary was less than a week away, and we'd come to England to both celebrate that and attend a massive game-software convention in hopes we'd network our way into finding a couple more people needed for the upcoming game. "So how could Asher help?"

"He knows what sorts of things to look for," Holder said darkly, then turned when a buxom blond woman poked her head into the room and told him if he wanted to take pictures of her in the new ale-wench costume, he'd better get to it, because she wasn't going to delay her goat yoga class for his silliness. "Ah, my sweet, the sun will never rise on a day when I don't wish to ogle your outstandingly fine form, with or without ale-wench ensemble. Yes, yes, I'll be right with you. Corb and Amy and I are just wrapping up our call."

"Sorry we're keeping him, although he made me try on the ale-wench costume last week, and after one look at me in it declared no one but you had the right stuff to dazzle players' eyes," I said with a cheerful wave at Holder's wife, Linda. She gave him a look fraught with meaning, wished Corbin and me a lovely visit and anniversary, and then retreated.

"I'll call Asher and see what he has to say," Holder said, frowning at something on one of his monitors. "Even if we don't get him involved in checking the code, he might have ideas. Speaking of hiring, how is the hunt going?"

"Not great," Corbin answered, watching me from the corners of his eyes. I could see that my nail down his spine had done much to put him in my state of mind, and he was clearly sending me smoldering looks that I had no trouble sending right back to him. "We liked one woman for heading up the engine tweaks, but she didn't seem any too keen on us."

"She made rude comments about California," I agreed, reaching behind Corbin to fondle what I could reach of his attractive ass.

He jumped slightly. "That is not in the least bit fair, Amy! I can't possibly grab your ass in response without Holder seeing that, and you know how it feeds his ego when he sees us pounce on each other."

"It does," Holder agreed without even glancing our way. "It makes me nigh on intolerable, according to Linda. What about the leads you got for the other two positions? Much though I want you two to have a good anniversary, we really need the team filled out."

"The con opens in two hours," Corbin said, making a grab for me when I slid off the bed and went to shake out the dress I planned to wear to the gaming developers' convention. "We'll do the best we can. I'm counting on Amy to make it clear just how wonderful it is to work for Buckling Swashes."

"Whereas I'm counting on Corbin's irresistible charm to sway people into signing on," I said from where I gathered up undergarments. I was out of view of the computer's camera, and held up my laciest bra. "But as he says, we'll do what we can. I guess I'll get dressed."

"The hell you will!" Corbin said, and added as he closed the laptop, "We'll talk later, Holder. Right now, I have a wife to appease."

Holder's laughter was cut off as the laptop switched into sleep mode. Corbin divested himself of the laptop, the sheets, and the sleeping shorts he habitually wore when traveling. I tossed my bra back onto my suitcase and sashayed my way over to where he was waiting, the light in his eyes making me feel like I was made of molten gold.

Corbin's eyes were truly the window to everything he was—kind, funny, charming, and far too sexy for his own good. All those facets of his being shone from within, and I never tired of simply being near him.

"I never get tired of you," I told him approximately an hour later, when we rode the elevator down to have a fast breakfast before heading to the convention.

"Thank you," he said gravely. "You keep me on my toes, too. I'm never one hundred percent sure what you're going to say or do."

"That's because I'm a woman of infinite depths," I told him without a single shred of modesty. "But also because I know you like quirky. Do you want to tackle the engineers, while I head up the interviews with the others?"

"Yes. And I'll be in meetings with the Chinese reps, don't forget."

We discussed our upcoming interviews, meetings, and press sessions while we hurriedly ate our way through what the Brits called a full English breakfast.

Four and a half hours later, I was drained, but stood up to greet the woman who had been escorted into one of the cubicles set up for companies hiring. "Hello. I'm Amy Monroe, CFO of Buckling Swashes. I'm afraid my husband was called into another meeting, but I'm happy to chat with you about the job."

"I'm sorry to miss your husband, but I'm pleased to meet you. I'm Emily Williams, soon to be Baxter."

"Getting married?" I asked, studying her. According to her résumé, she was in her early thirties, had a degree in physics, and enjoyed gaming with her partner. But beyond that, I liked the fact that she had laugh lines, and wore a tailored navy blue skirt and suit jacket but paired them with a faded Pride flag T-shirt.

"In eight days, yes," she said with a bright smile. "It's just a little wedding, really, with my parents, aunt and uncle, and a couple of friends. Fang and I—Fang is my fiancé—have a favorite hotel in a small town on the Cornwall coast. It's a hidden gem, but the owners are beyond amazing, and the walks around the area are outstanding, so much so that we try to visit once a year. Fang loves the big hill walks, so if you're into hiking, you're golden. Also, the town used to be fishing oriented, but now it's mostly given over to the visitors, since there is a long stretch of nice beach and a ton of rentals. Boy, I sound like I'm getting a kickback from the town council, huh?"

I laughed with her, and said a bit wistfully, "It sounds like the perfect venue, to be honest. Corbin and I were married at a judge's chambers, because we were caught in the middle of some legal issues with his former partner—business partner, not romantic—so we thought it would be best to get it over and done with so we could focus on restoring Buckling Swashes. In fact, our anniversary is two days before your wedding. I was hoping we could spend a little time in England to celebrate, but I'm not sure that will happen." I stopped myself from telling this stranger—nice as she seemed—the worry that something was awry with the new software.

Emily made a face. "I hate it when life gets in the way like that. Where were you planning on visiting? Because if you didn't have a destination, I can wholeheartedly recommend St. Gwynn. It's the cutest town, and you can go sailing, or hiking, and there's a stable that will take you out riding all day, and the shops are to die for. Honestly, if Fang's practice would let him move, I'd have us living there so fast his head would spin."

"It sounds ideal, it really does," I said, pulling out my phone. "What did you say the name was?"

She gave me the information on where the town was located, how to get to it by train, and even the name of the hotel she and her oddly named fiancé loved so much.

"Would you mind telling me why it is you are leaving your current company?" I asked, glancing again at her résumé. She'd listed what I assumed was a green power company as her employer.

"Sure. They're being sucked up into the mother ship." She gave a little laugh at the fact that my expression read confused. "Sorry, that's a little injoke. Vert Research is being acquired by an energy mega-conglomerate that we liken to a mother ship hoovering up all the smaller companies until there's no competition left. I don't want to work for a soulless corporation, so I've opted to take the leave package. Fang's bestie owns the company that organizes cons like this one, and he told me about Buckling Swashes joining the pool of those companies who are hiring. And since I like to game when I can, I thought it might be a good fit, jobwise."

Although she spoke with a breezy attitude, I didn't catch so much as a whiff of insincerity.

"I completely understand. Before I met Corbin and joined Buckling Swashes, I worked for an ecological group. It was frustrating due to all the misguided legislation, but satisfying at the same time," I told her.

"That's it, exactly," she said, smiling again. "There's a big gap between doing a job you like and doing a job you like that is making a difference in the world."

"Yeees," I drawled, not sure how to respond. "I don't know if our new game falls under the same 'benefitting the global population' umbrella as clean power, but ..."

To my relief, she chuckled at my lame attempt to justify a video game. "I know people who think that video games are utterly worthless, but really, they can do so much. They can connect people who are lonely or isolated, provide entertainment in a world that seems to grow more hopeless with every year, and if you get into puzzle games like Fang does, it hones cognitive abilities. I used to be able to beat him at word games, and now he wipes up the floor with me."

I laughed along with her, unable to keep from asking, "Fang is an unusual name. Is it a family tradition?"

"Kind of," Emily said with a wry smile. "His name is Francis, really, but he's been known as Fang since he got in his first tooth, when his mom used to say he looked like a baby vampire. What are you looking for from me?"

I blinked at the abrupt change of subject.

"Sorry," Emily apologized. "That was a big logic jump. I was curious about what sorts of skills you are looking for other than the few mentioned in the job listing."

"There's no need to apologize for being forthright—you're very like my daughter in that sense. As you have seen on the job posting, Buckling Swashes is creating a new Immersive Consciousness game. Corbin has a long, detailed explanation of what it is and how it works, but the end result is that it's basically the next generation of virtual reality. Because this model is unlike other software with this level of realism, we are concerned about breaking the suspension of disbelief if the physics of the world aren't right."

"That sounds fascinating," Emily said, her body language confirming her claim. "I'm not sure I understand what Immersive Consciousness is, though. I don't suppose you could tell me about it?"

"No," I said firmly, well aware that the fact Emily reminded me so much of my daughter, Tara, meant I was giving her a bit more license than I would any other interviewee. "I'm afraid that's proprietary information."

"Gotcha," she said, nodding. "I can tell you about my experience, if going beyond the CV will help."

"That would be perfect," I said, pulling out a notebook and pen to take notes. Corbin loved flipping me shit over the analog method I used to keep organized, but he never failed to buy me a fancy nibbed pen whenever he saw one he thought I'd like.

We discussed her education and job experience for the next ten minutes, and I whipped my way through the standard interview questions, all the while wishing Corbin were here with me. Similarity to Tara aside, I liked Emily a lot and thought she'd probably fit in well with the rest of the crew.

"I think we've talked about everything. Did you have any questions I haven't answered?" I asked her as I tucked away my notebook.

"Not really. I'll have to look into getting a high-speed Internet connection to handle all the work-from-home time, but that shouldn't be an issue."

"Dammit," I said, mentally calling myself a hundred names. "I'm so sorry, Emily, that 'dammit' was directed at me, not you. Just a few days ago, under recommendation of the graphics and programming heads, we decided that we couldn't send out units for our IC machines until development is further along. That means you'd be required to be in the office once a month for testing."

"Oh, man," she said, slumping back in the chair.

"Our job listing was updated to reflect that requirement, but perhaps you didn't see it?" I asked, fretting with my notebook.

"No, I didn't check it after my friend Devon told me there was a job that was perfect for me." She gave a big sigh and offered me a weak smile. "Well, that's that. I don't think a monthly commute to California is going to work out. Thank you for seeing me, and perhaps in the future …"

"Yes, absolutely," I said, feeling miserable. "Although … you know, before either of us makes a decision one way or the other, let me talk to Corbin. From your qualifications, and after meeting you, I think you'd work well with us. And as they say, never say never! If you are open to it, perhaps we can meet again, once Corbin and I can talk over the issue of travel."

Emily's expression went from regretful to stoic. "I would appreciate that. I'm not sure if something could be worked out, but if you're willing to leave the door open for discussion, then I'd love to be a part of that."

"Good. Let's put it on hold until Corbin and I can talk. Are you here in London for long?" We chatted for a few minutes before we both stood up. As we parted, I thanked her again for the recommendation for the Cornish hotel. "My husband wants us to visit Paris for a few days as soon as the convention is over, but we'll have a week after that, and I'm going to try to get us into your hotel."

"You'll love it," Emily said as she moved to the cubicle entrance, then paused, made a grimace, and added, "Although you won't be able to get a reservation around my wedding day. People who are there for the wedding can stay the day before, during, and after. Although …"

"Although?" I said, flipping through the calendar on my phone, hoping against hope that I'd magically find some extra time for Corbin and me to be tourists.

"OK, this …" She hesitated, then said with a little shake of her head, "… this is going to sound a little crazy, I know, but if you really wanted to stay at Foxglove and Nightshade while my family and friends are sucking up the space, you could tell the owners of the hotel you were there for the wedding. My family is only going to take up seven of the eight rooms, so you might as well grab the remaining one rather than letting it go to waste."

"Oh, we wouldn't feel at all comfortable invading the hotel during your wedding," I said, disappointment making my voice sharper than I liked. "We'd feel like we were crashing it."

"Pfft," she said, to my surprise waving away the idea. "It's really not a big deal. It's just the two of us, a couple of friends, and a handful of family. To be honest, it's more about the result than the act, if you know what I mean."

I couldn't stop myself from making a lightning-swift glance at her midsection.

"No, not that. Visas," Emily said, laughing when I started stammering out apologies. She cut them short with a, "That's what everyone who doesn't know us thinks. Fang and I aren't the kid sort of people. If my sister ever reproduces, we'll be the fun aunt and uncle, but as for kids of our own? Eh. I'd rather have animals."

My cheeks were still warm from embarrassment, but she clearly was not offended, so I tried to put the shame behind me. "I'm with you on that, although I do admit to having a child, a daughter who is now in her midtwenties, and the person everyone at Buckling Swashes fears, including Corbin and me."

"Ah?" Emily asked, looking a bit confused.

"Sorry, I'm joking about my daughter, Tara. She works with the game engineers, and keeps everyone on their toes because she loves the company so much."

"Gotcha," Emily said. "I'm serious about the offer to say you're part of the wedding group, in case you thought I'm either trying to butter you up for a job or deranged. Or both."

"I appreciate that," I said after a moment of warring with my inner self. I really wanted to have a romantic getaway with Corbin, and I was under no illusions that Emily would be the least bit interested in what a couple of middle-aged people were doing, although I was cognizant she might be doing it with an ulterior motive in mind.

I didn't really think that was the situation, however. She seemed too genuine.

In the end, I decided to go with my gut instinct. "And I think I will take you up on it, if you are absolutely certain it wouldn't be an imposition."

"Not in the least," she answered, and gave me the exact dates the hotel would be limited to her wedding party.

"We might get done in Paris early, so we wouldn't need to intrude, but assuming that things take longer than I expect, I will go ahead and book the room during your event. You will, naturally, allow us to give you a wedding gift."

"Oh, hell, no!" she exclaimed, then covered her mouth to stifle the resulting laughter that followed the several heads swiveling to look at us. She gave an apologetic moue to everyone in the room, then told me, "I appreciate the thought, but we're doing charity donations only for the wedding. If you really feel obligated to me, feel free to make a donation to whatever animal charity you like."

"You really do prefer animals to people," I said, referring to the statement she'd made earlier.

"Fang is a vet, and yes, we both love the beasties. Hopefully, I'll see you again!" she said as we walked to the elevator. "It was a pleasure to meet you."

"Likewise, and yes, hopefully we'll see you around the hotel."

The rest of the day dragged without Corbin, who had been whisked away by a group of programmers whom he'd known since his college days, but at last we met after dinner, and I told him all about Emily.

"It's a shame she can't do the commute, but Ben would have my balls if I sent one of the units out of the country," Corbin said when I finished. "He says no amount of NDAs would cover the risk we'd take until the system is further along."

"Tell your lawyer your balls are mine," I said, eyeing the room service menu. Although I'd had dinner with some of Corbin's software buddies, he had been tied up with yet another potential foreign investor, and since he was infinitely more charming than me, I was happy to take a nap and a long soak in the tub before he finally rolled into the room. "Metaphorically speaking, of course."

"Of course," he replied. He pursed his lips as he watched me.

"You want something, too? I didn't get much dinner because your buddies insisted on going to sushi, and you know how raw fish squicks me out. I'm thinking a nice, unhealthily rich and completely not-on-my-diet steak pie."

"I've told you that there is not one single thing about you that I don't equally love and lust after," he said, clearly throwing grammar to the wind.

"And I've told you that sort of attitude would win you any woman in the world, but since I am not letting you go for anything, you may eat the mushy peas that comes with the steak pie."

We had recently discovered that for some inexplicable reason, Corbin had a passion for British mushy peas. His eyes lit. "Will you let me eat them off of you?"

I lowered the menu again to assess the statement. "Possibly. I'd have to see what they felt like on my skin, first. You wouldn't rather lick chocolate off me?"

He nodded toward the bed. "Do you really want to leave chocolate-colored smears on the bedding?"

"Oh, hell no. I would die of embarrassment if the hotel staff thought we were scatological sorts of people. But, that said, I don't want green mushy pea stains on the sheets, either."

Corbin heaved a big sigh, and peeled off his shirt in preparation to taking a fast shower. "All right, but don't tell me later that I didn't fulfill your every sexual fantasy just because you were afraid of a little mushy pea stain. No, I don't want steak … but I would take a burger. A big one. Dinner seems like it was days ago."

"You are an odd man, but luckily, I like odd," I called after him, placed our room service order, then sat back on the bed, and looked again at the confirmation message from the hotel. I really wanted Corbin to meet Emily, and although she would no doubt be very busy with her wedding and family, perhaps I could arrange for a brief meeting, one where he would see the same potential that I saw in her.

I wasn't sure if there was a way we could manage having her employed without being asked to visit the office monthly, but I had a feeling in the pit of my stomach that it would be a good thing to try to work out.

I smiled as I looked again at the hotel's website pictures. Regardless of the situation with Emily's employment, I very much looked forward to getting Corbin away from all the industry people.

We were going to honeymoon like it was 2005.

FOUR
BIG GLITTER IS OUT TO GET YOU

EMILY
August 6th

The land rolled out before me like an undulating, lush green-and-gold patchwork. I leaned against the massive rock that crowned the hill known locally as Gwenyvere's Bower despite the fact that there was nothing bower-like about the rocky outcropping, and considered my life.

"Thus far, it's been going well. But I don't like not having a job," I said aloud to no one, the August breeze whipping away my words, but not before they were overheard.

"You got canned? You can come work for us," a voice said behind me.

Bess panted her way to the top of the Bower, her hair stuffed into a knit cap despite the warmth of the day. She looked like a middle-aged hipster, if such a thing was possible, and I studied my older sister with the eye of one who saw her roughly once a year.

"You look good," I said, wanting to point out that I could see some silver in her dirty blond hair. "Happy. Satisfied. Fulfilled."

Her lips twisted. "Hardly that when we have Big Glitter on our ass."

"Really?" I leaned out to look at the seat of her pants. "Did you sit on it?"

"Oh lord, your sense of humor. I forgot about it," she answered in response, making shooing motions until I shifted down the rock a few feet, so she could lean against it and catch her breath.

"Who or what is Big Glitter?" I couldn't help but ask.

"The companies that are after those of us who are working to ban nonbiodegradable glitter. Stop making that face; it is a serious subject!"

"I know it is, but I badly want to make a joke about a glitter bomb," I admitted, unable to keep from nudging her with my elbow.

She rolled her eyes. "How do you find that funny? I suppose since you are a bride, I'll have to put up with your flippancy, but for the love of all that's good in this world, try to keep a firm grip on it."

"Are you kidding?" I went back to contemplating the view. "My quirky nature is what endears me to people, or so says Fang. Where's Monk?"

"Trying to locate the safe house to which we've been assigned for the next four days." She narrowed her eyes on me. "You're sure we couldn't stay with you—"

"Our landlady is very nosy and is always watching us. She's nice, and we like her, but if we're out in the yard, she always wants to chat. So if you are trying to keep a low profile, then I would suggest finding somewhere else."

She sighed with all the drama of a reality-TV actor. "Fine, but if we get caught, I'm hitting you up for bail money first. So, the wedding is on the eighteenth?"

"Yup." I confirmed the place and hotel. "Mom insisted we hold a room for you, but if you don't think you'd be safe there …" I let the sentence trail off. I had kind of an odd relationship with my sister, given her dedication to whatever ecological or animal-rights abuse caught her fancy. I was certain she was making a change for the better, but it didn't make it any easier to be around her.

"Hmm. That's a good question." She chewed it over for a few minutes while I took pictures of the patchwork fields. "Go ahead and keep the room for us. I'm sure we weren't clocked when we slipped into England, so there's no way any of them will find us for one night at a small, out-of-the-way hotel. You're paying, right?"

"Yes, I told Mom we'd pay for the hotel stay, but you're on your own after that night. We're not made of money, especially since I'm now unemployed, and no one wants to hire me. Thank god for Fang."

"Mm-hmm," she said, now abstracted by her phone. "Oh good, Monk found the place. Right. I'll see you on the seventeenth or eighteenth, assuming the coven doesn't get word I'm back in England."

She started to leave, but I caught her arm and stopped her. "You can't possibly just walk off after an exit line like that."

"That's what good exit lines are for," she argued, and tried to pry my hand off her arm.

I tightened my fingers until she glared at me. "Yes, and now you will explain what coven you're talking about, and why they would be interested in knowing you're in England. Did you become a Wiccan?"

"No, hedge witch. Vigilante hedge witch, actually." She rustled around in her bag, and pulled out a pewter pentagram pin, which she handed me. "Here, you can use this for your something borrowed. The coven doesn't believe in what they termed as being militant activities, and said they'll formally de-witch me. Ha! Like I'm going to allow them do that? There's far too much at stake to let them stifle our work. Gotta run. Monk says he's coming back to pick me up so we can meet with an informant who says we are needed to shut down a particularly heinous cockfighting group."

"Wow," I said, more than a little amazed by Bess. "There's a lot to unpack there, but let's start with the big one: vigilante hedge witch? Aren't hedge witches just people learned in the lore of the surrounding countryside? Herbalists and that sort of thing? Where does the vigilante element enter into it?"

"Someone has to make sure people treat Gaia the way she deserves to be treated. If they don't, that's where I come in," Bess said darkly, then, without another word, trotted down the hill to the path below that led to a small car park.

"I think it can be said that I have the weirdest family," I told the view; then with a sigh at having to bear the burden of being the only sane one in the fam, I made my way down the rocky track.

When I got home, I was surprised to see Fang's car next to the house, since I knew he had meetings with the clinic partners.

"Just so you know, my sister has officially gone beyond wacky and into the land of outright bonkers. Er. You OK?" I asked when I entered the house and found Fang flat out on the couch with Tristan, the three-legged black cat we'd rescued a few months before, spread across his chest. Between his feet, Chloe, a nearly deaf, elderly border collie mix, was curled into a tight brown, black, and white ball.

"I've always thought of your sister as borderline deranged, so this news doesn't come as a shock to me," he said, flailing one free arm for a moment.

"No, no, I wouldn't dream of disturbing you so I can actually snuggle with the man I'm going to marry in a few short days. You two stay right there and hog all the Fang," I told the animals, neither of whom had so much as glanced up at me when I entered.

Fang laughed when I plopped down onto the floor next to him. "You know I will happily divest myself of all animals to provide you with snuggling."

"I know," I said, waving away the offer. "Just as I know that the animals don't actually dislike me. It's just that they—like every other animal we come in contact with—like you so much *more* than me. It's not fair! I like them as much as you do, but all I get is a little cuddle on the lap whenever they think they can mooch food off me. It's maddening that you're some sort of animal whisperer, and I'm a far-distant second best."

This was an old complaint, and one I trotted out whenever I felt ignored by the animals, but both of us knew it had no real bite to it.

Fang laughed again, but this time managed to remove both animals in order to pull me up onto the couch so I was lying half across him, his hands on my butt as I nibbled along his jaw.

"Oooh," I said, squirming a little when his hands went wandering. "Are we going to have sexy times? Because if so, we need to close the curtains. You know how Mrs. Fliss drops by without warning."

Fang gave the living room window a long look but, after a moment's thought, sighed and retrieved his hands from where they were divesting me of my leggings. "Normally, I'd take you up on that offer, not that I want to try the sofa again after last time when you tried that fancy dismount and ended up breaking your toe on the coffee table. But we need to talk first."

"Uh-oh," I said, sitting up when I caught edges of anger and something more troubling in his tone. Was it fear? I gave a mental shake of the head. Fang was, as a rule, a cautious man where I tended to leap, then look, but at the same time, he was extraordinarily brave. He frequently tackled animals and situations that others refused, never once putting his own safety over his oath to protect and aid animals. "I don't like the sound of that. I take it the partners had something to say to you guys?"

"You could say that."

I slid off his lap, allowing him to sit next to me on the couch. He rested his elbows on his knees and watched as Tristan pounced on Chloe's tail, leaving me with a sudden soggy feeling in the pit of my stomach.

"What is it?" I asked, leaning into him. "Say it quickly, like you're ripping off a bandage."

Fang sighed again, then leaned back, wrapping around me. "As of the start of September, I will be without employment."

"What?" The screech was so loud that not only did Tristan go into FRAP mode and tear off to race around the bedrooms, but Chloe actually heard it and rolled one eyeball in my direction.

Fang flinched, and rubbed his ear.

"I'm so sorry," I apologized, on my knees next to him to hold a hand over his ear. "I didn't realize I could make that sort of a noise, let alone in that volume. Did I blast out your earball?"

"Yes, but I still love you, and I don't think any lasting damage was done," he answered, taking my hand so he could give his head a quick shake, just like I'd blasted his ear parts around. "Although I know exactly how you feel. When Nickerson announced that all twelve of us in the county clinics are being let go, pretty much everyone was stunned."

"Why are they firing you? Wait … there's only four of you vets at your clinic. You, Ned Nickerson—"

"John Nickerson, but yes, Nancy Drew, continue on," Fang said, curling one side of his mouth up in a way that made me want to kiss him all over his delightful face.

"—Dr. Monica, and Hamish," I finished. "Oh man, poor Hamish! He just got hired, too. I hope he isn't going to blame your mentorship for this."

"I don't think he will, not that one thing is related to the other." He ran a hand over his face, and I felt another slop of the wet, clammy feeling in my stomach. "And because I know you're going to ask, no, no one did anything wrong. There were no complaints, no problem with clients, nothing but one corporation deciding to buy out a competitor, then eliminate the latter."

"Someone bought out Fangs, Fur, and Wings?" I asked, naming the small company that owned a scattering of vet clinics around the west of England. "And fired the vets who make the company work?"

"The owners sold the company to Veterinary Excellence, yes," he said.

I flinched at the name of the mega-company that owned vet clinics all over the UK and western Europe. They were known for their high prices, upsell tactics, and control of vet drug research. "That absolutely blows. Are they going to close the FFW clinics?"

"Nickerson said they will consolidate clinics, but fill them with VE people." He sighed and gave me a smile so filled with rue, it made me want to hold him tight against the ills of the world. "The partners will remain, but those of us who are average, run-of-the-mill vets are off with a month's severance."

I curled into him, feeling him so warm and solid and wonderfully Fang that it brought tears to my eyes. "It'll be OK. Everyone says vets are in short supply. You'll find another place, one that won't sell you to the highest bidder."

"With eleven other vets hitting the market at the same time?" It took him a few seconds, but he shook his head. "There's only so many vets needed. Hamish said he was thinking about going back to Canada, since the need demand outstrips supply. But I won't borrow trouble, as my mother used to say. Besides, there's no reason to be doom and gloom about an impoverished future when you are being wooed by prestigious software companies. How did the interview go?"

I stared at him for a moment, my stomach now evidently filled with lumpy, cold porridge. Spoiled cold porridge. "It went well. The CFO said I could have the job if I wanted."

Fang watched me closely, his expression going from hopeful and proud to clouded. "Did you take it?"

I shook my head, swallowing hard. "They said I'd have to commute once a month for a couple of days in order to use their proprietary equipment. I told them flying from England to California every month wasn't going to work for us. Oh, god, Fang. What are we going to do? We can't both be out of a job at the same time. We have animals to support! And Mrs. Fliss depends on our rent. The Eltons depend on her. We can't ruin everyone's lives just because the world suddenly decided we should be jobless!"

Fang must have heard the crack in my voice, because he tugged me tighter against him, and rubbed my back in the best "vet calming a startled animal" manner. "It's all right, Em. It may seem like we're under a dark cloud right now, but it's not permanent. We'll get through this like we have everything else."

I looked up at him, sniffling a little. "With grace and aplomb?"

"With a good deal of sweaty bunny-lovin' sex," he said.

"You smooth talker, you!" I said, pulling his T-shirt off over his head.

With a manly chuckle, he reciprocated by peeling various garments off me, and scattered them hither and yon as we made our way to the bedroom.

My parents called the next day just before lunch.

"Emily, your father has something to say to you," Mom announced in her best community theater voice, the one clearly audible not only in the back of the auditorium but out in the parking lot, and sometimes, when she was particularly focused, all the way to the drive-thru of a nearby fast-food place. "Something impactful. I want you to weigh his words well, and not be swayed by either the bonds of paternal affection that you may hold for him or your love of all things mystery. Brother? You know what to do."

There was the sound of someone handing her phone to my father, followed by muffled footsteps retreating and the overly loud slamming of a door.

"Someone's in trouble with Mom," I told Brother, idly watching Mrs. Fliss as she hobbled around her minuscule front garden. "What did you do now?"

"Exist?" he asked, sotto voce.

Evidently, it wasn't as *sotto* as he hoped, because, "TELL HER!" could be heard even through the closed door.

I giggled.

"You may well laugh, but it's you that has me in this situation," Brother said, breathing heavily through his nose for a few minutes before his leather chair made farting noises as he sat down. "And much though I'd like to demand you accommodate me, your mother has a point. You are my youngest child. You are being married. I, as your doting, if not uncritical, paternal figure, should be there."

"What's this? Why are you making a big deal about being at the wedding? I told you I don't mind if you aren't around the whole time." I scooted the cat out of my seat and plopped down, only to immediately have a dog curl up on my feet, and Tristan, with a little side stink eye at me usurping the comfy chair, settled himself on my lap. "It's all copacetic, Brother."

"No, it's not." He breathed heavily for another few seconds before adding, "The schedule for the tour just came in. The tour of Conan Doyle's house is the same day as your wedding. The tea with the relative will take up that afternoon. As your mother said, I know my duty."

"Wait a second," I said, absently petting the cat and wiggling my toes where Chloe dug her elbow into them.

"I'm not going to say I haven't thought of canceling the whole tour," Brother continued, martyrdom leaching from his words. "It's a once-in-a-lifetime event, but so is a daughter getting married. Except you could marry again, and I doubt if the Conan Doyle relative has many teas with historians, but still, that's life."

"What do you want me to say?" I asked, amused. Mom always said I was so much like Brother, she was a bit insulted that her genes counted for little. I discounted that complaint for years, but since Fang once told me how like Brother I was, I'm a bit more willing to admit that we might share a few quirky traits. "That you don't have to come to my wedding?"

"No, of course not. I wouldn't dream of asking such a thing." He was silent for a moment; then he gave a soulful sigh, and his voice dropped to a tone I knew meant he was speaking from the heart. "I couldn't miss your wedding. We may not always agree about things, but you are my little Emily, and I love you and owe it to you to be there on your big day."

Tears pricked painfully behind my eyes. Brother hadn't called me little Emily since I was five or six. "I love you, too, but you know, being a father doesn't mean you have to sacrifice your own life for mine."

"I rather think that is exactly the description of being a parent," he said, but his voice had lightened a bit.

"That may be for other families, but we are Williamses, and we are not like normal people."

"You can say that again. What? Yes, I told her!" The last part was clearly yelled to Mom.

"How about this—and don't say no, because we both know I don't take well to being told I can't do things unless there's a really logical reason for it— how about you attend the tour and tea, and pop in afterward? You'll miss the actual ceremony, but it's not going to be a big deal."

"I couldn't!" he protested, and to give him credit, I didn't even hear a thread of regret in his voice. "I couldn't miss the ceremony."

My heart warmed at the fact that he was truly willing to give up a dream day just to see Fang and me say a few words and sign a legal document. I sniffled softly to myself, and chalked my errant emotions up to hormones. "Brother, do you even know me? I'd totally toss over my own wedding to tour the house and have the tea."

"I couldn't," he repeated a third time, but this time slower.

"You absolutely could, you know. I wouldn't mind in the least. I know Mom will kick up a bit of a fuss, but it's my wedding, and if I say you don't have to be there, then that's the way it is."

"But … I have to walk you down the aisle," he protested. "Your mother had my tux taken out. Not that I've gained weight—the tux must have shrunk since the last time I wore it. But it's there and ready to be worn."

"You can wear it at the after-party. As for the other, Fang and I are going to walk each other down the aisle," I said, making a snap decision. I truly did not care about the ceremony; the main reason we were having a wedding to begin with was as an excuse to have family and friends visit. It's why our focus was on the pre- and postceremony events. "Brother, listen to me: I want you to do the Conan Doyle house. I want you to have tea with the relative. I want you to tell the relative that your daughter grew up reading Sherlock Holmes, and that you got me started on a lifelong love of mysteries. You do that, and Fang and I will get married, and then when the tea is over, you join the party afterward. OK?"

"I couldn't do that. It wouldn't be right," he said, but this time, I heard a little bit of hesitancy.

It took five more minutes of me swearing up one side and down the other that I really, truly did not mind if he wasn't present for the actual ceremony, and then once he accepted the truth, and gratefully thanked me for thinking of him when I should be focused on myself, I had to repeat the whole thing over again for Mom.

"Well, I think this is just wrong, but you always were one to do things your own way," Mom finally said.

I was worried for a moment that she was genuinely upset, but after fifteen minutes of solid reassurance that it made no difference to me, she acquiesced.

"I suppose Brother could watch the video of the ceremony as soon as he gets to the hotel, so he'll be up to speed," she finished. "As it is, I'm going to have to leave two days afterward for the Neo-Pict course. I told you about their silversmithing class, yes? I hope to make some lovely brooches for you and Bess. Would you prefer one with a bull head, or a ram?"

"Definitely the sheep," I told her. "Although I'd love a wolf if you guys get to do those."

"I'll ask. If nothing else, I can make the ram brooch for Fang. It'll look lovely on him when he's out drenching all those sheep."

"Uh-huh," I said, hesitating, then deciding not to mention the approaching lack of employment in the

Williams-Baxter home. "I heard from Bess, by the way. She's going to try to make it to the wedding, but I have to say I think she's gone off the deep end."

"More than normal?" Brother asked, since Mom had put the phone on speaker, her attention having wandered off now that the situation was resolved. "We really should have had someone look at her when she was a child, Chris."

"We should have had both girls evaluated," I could hear Mom say from what was no doubt the opposite side of the room, where she had a small desk. "Neither one of them were normal, but that comes from your side."

"I resent that accusation," Brother said. "There is nothing wrong with my family."

A pregnant silence fell from both England and Washington.

"Nothing serious," he amended. "Not with the immediate family. The others are a bit ... different. My father was exceedingly normal, so any strangeness in the family must come from another source. Although, my sister did run off to live in the wilds of Scotland with a mad Scot, so perhaps it's just me who is the sane one."

"Bah. Iain is not mad in the least," I said, pulling my laptop over so I could see it. I loaded up the employment company that I'd hired to find me a new job, but there wasn't anything new to pursue. "He's just very much a farmer. Fang says he has extremely sound agricultural practices."

"And there can be no higher praise," Brother murmured.

"Damn straight. Right, are we done? Because I want to take a nap, and the cat is purring like crazy, and Chloe is dreaming about chasing rabbits."

"You're sure—" Brother started to say.

"Five hundred percent sure. You know me. You know how I feel about marriage. This is not a big deal. I would be very angry if I thought you'd miss seeing ACD's house and relative. Just be sure to take lots of pictures, and maybe you could have the relative sign a napkin or something for me."

Brother agreed to doing what he could, and hung up.

That night, when Fang came home, I told him what had transpired.

"I know you don't care much about the ceremony itself," he said as we fixed spaghetti together. "But I worry that you will regret not having Henry at the actual wedding."

"Dude," I told him, and popped a piece of garlic bread into his mouth. "You know me better than anyone. This is Sir Arthur Conan Doyle we're talking about."

Even though he didn't have the same love of mysteries as Brother and me, he agreed that it would be a shame to miss the Conan Doyle event.

Later, when we were spooned in bed (Fang and I took turns in being the big spoon), Fang was breathing into my hair, his body relaxing as he drifted into sleep. I lay on my side, watching through the window as the moon started to rise over a line of windbreak trees, casting an eerie light over the familiar fields of the pasture.

"What would you think of moving to the States?"

For a few seconds, I thought I was dreaming, but then I rolled onto my back and looked at Fang. His eyes were on me, and although it was too dark to see the expression in them, I knew he was about to make a sacrifice for me. "You mean to move back so I can take the Buckling Swashes job? It might not be necessary, not if we could work out a way for me to fly to California less often than once a month."

"In the worst-case scenario, then. Assuming they would offer you the job if the travel wasn't an issue?"

That was a question, and I knew what he was hinting at.

"I think they'd offer me the job, yes," I told him, going back over my interview with Amy. "We agreed to leave it on a 'we'll talk later' level, so assuming I didn't misread her response, I think a job offer is possible."

"Would you like going back to the States?" he asked again, his breath brushing my face. I smooshed myself against his gorgeous, naked, warm chest.

"Yes. But moving means you leaving your home."

"You left your home for me. Maybe it's my turn to do the same for you."

I sat up and clicked on the light, needing to see him if we were going to have this sort of a talk. He blinked a few times, and I couldn't help but reach out and brush the rich brown hair out of his eyes. "You mean it, don't you?"

"Yes." His gaze was steady on mine.

"But … what would you do?" I asked, considering the idea. To be honest, I wouldn't mind at all tackling that job, since it sounded fascinating and would add to my skill set. But it wasn't all about me.

"Get a job," he answered, then rolled onto his back, pulling me down with him. "I'll have to take a qualifying exam to practice in the US, but I asked Nickerson, and he said I can do that in England, and that he'd do what he could to help me find a job in California."

"Not California," I said slowly, thinking about it.

"Washington?" he asked.

"Yes." I tipped my head back and gently bit him on his chin.

He pinched me on my ass.

"Your parents?"

"They're getting older," I said, thinking furiously. "If we moved within an hour or two from them—not close, but not out of reach—then if they need us, we could help out. And flying to California from Seattle is a whole lot easier than from England."

Fang thought about that for a few minutes. "That would work. I'll get the application form for the exam tomorrow, and see what I'll need to get qualified in the States."

For the first time since Fang had told me about the layoff, I felt a spurt of hope. "We can come back here as frequently as possible. I'd hate to not see our friends again. Devon travels a lot, but you know how Holly is. It's almost impossible to get her off the commune."

"There's nothing to say we can't return to England to live at a later date," Fang said, one arm around me as we settled again.

I liked that idea. "We could do five years in the US, then come back here for five years," I said, more than a little excited at the idea of both a new start and the financial stability that came with us being gainfully employed. Fang and I had talked about starting an animal sanctuary one day, and that took oodles of money. "Or ten years. Or, hell, whatever time frame we feel like. Fang! This is such a good idea. You would be OK living in the US?"

"I lived in Canada for four years, so it's not like the culture shock will kill me," he pointed out.

We talked late into the night, but in the morning, we both felt better about our situations.

I just hoped the good feelings would prove to be valid.

FIVE
THE MORNING BEFORE
THE DAY AFTER

EMILY
August 17th

"Your family's outside," Fang said the morning of Wedding Eve. He staggered past us bearing two wheelie suitcases, with two more stuffed under his arms. "Hullo, Holly. Is there a reason your wife is hiding in the back of your car?"

"She's talking to her mom," Holly said as I released her from a mammoth hug. "Her therapist told her to only do so when she can get into a fetal position."

Fang paused on the way to the short polished oak bar that served as a registration desk. We both looked at Holly.

"It's kind of a long story," she said with a wry smile. "And one not really suitable for mixed company."

"Ah," was all Fang said before dropping the luggage, and, with a twitch of his lips that indicated he was highly amused, returned to the small parking area outside the hotel.

Holly beamed at me as she held me at arm's length. "You both look happy and healthy and almost, but not quite, as much in love as Marla and me. Oh, Em—I'm so happy to be here."

I gave her another hug, one arm around her as we turned to face the group of people entering the lobby. "As if I could get married without you here to see? Mom, really, how much luggage did you bring?"

My mother bustled forward dragging another wheeled suitcase, followed immediately by my aunt Kathie, teen cousin Clara, and Iain and Fang.

"This one's empty. It's for the things we'll pick up and ship home. Oh, hello. Yes, I'm Mrs. Williams. Your hotel is just darling! No wonder Emily and Fang love it here. Do you need my passport?"

"Emily, my dear, you are positively radiant!" Aunt Kathie told me. "Holly, it's lovely to see you again. Is that your wife in the boot of your car? She appeared to be doing some Zen meditation thing. We thought it best to let her be."

"Oh dear. If her mom drove her into meditating—" Holly hurried off to check on her wife of almost ten years.

"Is something wrong?" Kathie asked, glancing toward the door. "Should I not have mentioned it?"

"Not at all. Marla is kick-ass in every area of life except her mom. She's a black belt, you know. Marla, not her mom."

"The woman in the car? Isn't she a shearer?" Iain had limped over to where we stood, Fang obviously having wrestled away from him their luggage. "Emily, love, you look radiant."

"I already said that," Kathie said, grinning at him.

"Great minds," he said with faux solemnity, and moved over to the desk where Mom was chatting with Mace Abbot, the hotel owner, about the sights in the area.

"Thank you both for the compliment, and yes, Marla shears sheep and alpacas and some goats. She's a marvel, and I don't just say that because she has a platonic crush on Fang."

The man himself, who moved over to join our conversation circle, gave a little roll of his eyes before he wrapped an arm around my waist. I leaned into him. "It's just because I'm a vet who specializes in sheep, and am madly in love with a woman who would geld me if I so much as flicked an eyelash toward another female. How's your farm going, Iain? No signs of fluke your way?"

"None, thank the lord," Iain said, and the two men moved to the side where a couple of love seats sat, immediately going into sheep-chat mode.

"Why is Iain limping?" I asked Kathie when she waved Iain toward the seats and headed for Mace.

"Knee surgery. Tell you about it later. Hello, we're the MacLarens. We have two connecting rooms."

"Dad fell off the mountain," Clara said, not glancing up from her phone.

"That sucks," I answered, eyeing her. I figured she was just another teen addicted to her phone, but she looked up at that and blinked at me. "You look good. How're the goats going?"

"Excellent. This year, we've tried a new formula, and I think it's going to be a success. Mum said it would be nice if I did a soap for you and Fang." She tapped on her phone and held it up to me, displaying a photo of a bar of soap. It was a pale cream with two pink fingers poked up in the peace sign.

"Oh, cool," I said, pleased by the gesture. "That was thoughtful of you to go to all that work for us. Did your mom tell you that I used to always flash the peace sign when I was around your age?"

"No," she said, looking back at her phone. "It's you and Fang holding hands. Or rather, it's your arms holding hands."

"Oh, gotcha," I said, feeling like a boob. I studied the soap. "That is a very sweet gesture. Thank you."

"We brought you some," she said, before turning to join her dad. "It's called Emily and Fang Get Married. People on Insta are crazy for it. We're on our fourth batch."

"Mom," I said quietly when my mother paused next to me, tucking her wallet and passport away in her bag. "Please tell me I was never that eccentric."

My mother may be the queen of diving into her interest du jour with a focus that leaves her unaware of everything else, but she's not stupid, nor does she lack anything when it comes to astuteness. "No," she said, giving the lobby a quick once-over. I relaxed. "You were far, far worse."

"I was not!" I protested, wanting to be outraged but not quite able to pull it off.

"You most definitely were, and before you argue the point, please recall your twenty-first birthday when you presented your father and me with copies of what you referred to as your biography to that point."

The memory of the book I'd pulled together containing a series of emails, texts, and journal entries of my late teen years—and the adventures that had happened to me—rose with horrible clarity.

"That was more than ten years ago," I said, refusing to acknowledge the memory.

"And there's the fact that even at the pinnacle of your shenanigans, you didn't make money hand over fist, like Clara. Fang, dear, did you see a striped bag the size of a bulldog—oh, thank you."

"I shenaniganned in poverty," I told Fang when he returned to my side.

"Really?" he asked, his forehead wrinkling.

"OK, it wasn't poverty, but I'm not going to be a millionaire at fifteen as evidently my cousin is," I said, ignoring grammar to make my point.

Fang's brows rose above the forehead wrinkles. "The goat's-milk-soap market is doing that well?"

"Evidently." We both turned when a short burst of music came from the parking lot.

"Oh lord," Mom said, passing a dramatic hand over her brow. I made a mental note to ask if she'd joined up with another production by the local drama group. "It's Brother. Emily, I meant to warn you, but I hoped he'd get better."

"What's wrong?" I asked, fear hitting me in the same spot that went cold and clammy. "Is Brother ill?"

"No. It's far worse than that." Mom turned her head in what I'm sure she thought was expressing a form of noble martyrdom. "He's become Detective Inspector Mortimer of the CID."

"Huh?" I asked, my stomach happily returning to its normal—if a bit empty—warm state.

"It's the tour," Mom said, diving into her bag again. "It's his persona."

"All the people are assigned a character to 'play' during the tour," Fang told me, showing me a text on his phone. It was from Brother, and included a photo of a crossword puzzle, with a request for help on the circled item.

"I am now DI Mortimer of the CID. None of the others are actual police, and two of my colleagues are insanely jealous. Do you know about those places that hand out lorddoms, and if so, how much they charge? Also, do I have to get the title in my name, or could I get it in the name of Mortimer? I think one or two of the people on the tour would crap their metaphysical pants if I rolled up at breakfast and announced I was now a lord," I read aloud. I looked up at Fang.

His lips twitched.

"If you tell me I'm like him one more time, I'm going to punch you," I said with a narrowed eye before giving him back his phone.

"Really?" He waggled his eyebrows at me. "Do I get to pick where you punch me?"

"See?" I said, pointing at him. "You're every bit as weird as me. Mom, did Brother get a costume to go with his alter ego? Because so help me, if he got a Victorian policeman's uniform and did not get me a street urchin's outfit, I may well ban him from the reception."

"Street urchin's outfit?" Holly asked, having returned to the lobby. "You're not wearing the dress you showed me?"

"Not for the wedding," I said, and quickly explained the latest insanity concerning my father.

"Why do you want to be dressed like a Victorian street urchin?" she asked, looking confused.

I gawked at her, outright gawked. "How can you have known me for sixteen years and not known about my lifelong desire to cosplay as a plucky Victorian street urchin whom is swept away by a dashing but slightly dangerous, yet extremely affluent, British gentleman, with whom she later sets up a successful thievery school to benefit all the other urchins and unhoused people?"

"The first is 'who,' not 'whom,' and who is the affluent—"

"Fang, of course!" I said, giving her a look.

"If Fang is the cohort in your role-play fantasy, then it can hardly have been a lifelong desire, since you've only known him as long as me," she answered, her eyebrows arched.

I arched mine in response, realized how idiotic that probably made me look (my eyebrows are not my strong point), and returned them to their normal position before saying, "There are times when I think you took your Buddhist nun vows far too seriously, Holly Alton-Mayer, and this is one of those times."

She giggled. "I don't recall taking a vow to point out when you were exaggerating, but if I did, then I apologize for being so unthinking. Besides, I left that life to be with Marla."

"You're still a layperson Buddhist, and more importantly, an instigator," I told her, giving her another hug. Just seeing her again filled me with so much happiness I worried I might burst out into a song at any moment. "But luckily, it's one of your charms."

"I've never instigated in my life," she said, laughing now, stopping only when Fang—who had gone out to the parking lot, no doubt to help whoever needed it—entered the hotel with the tall, dark-haired, blue-eyed man who set hearts aflutter in more locations than I could name.

"Devon!" Holly and I squealed at the same time; then we were in a three-way hug with our old friend, and Fang's best man.

"I was never that young," Iain told Kathie as Holly and I did a little jig of happiness at seeing Devon.

"I don't think I've ever hopped around like that for a man, especially one who isn't my husband," she answered.

He gave her a long look. "Would ye hop fer me if I was askin' ye to?" His accent, which was normally quite understandable, went full Highlander.

"That depends." She leaned in close to him. "What would you be wearing while I was doing all the hopping?"

I stopped my Devon happy dance and sent my aunt a look. "If I can't PDA with Fang, per Brother's explicit request, then you have to keep your kinky role-play talk to a dull roar." I thought for a moment, then added, "All right, I might be interested in this whole hopping and Scotsman scenario, but only because Fang does a really good Scottish accent. So go ahead, but don't say anything that would shock Mom."

"Oh, I'm fine," Mom said, moving off to greet Marla, Holly's wife, when she entered. "The Picts had a philosophy of live and let live, and I think we as a society have strayed away from that for too long. Marla, what a pleasure it is to see you again."

"I don't think the Picts were known for that at all," Holly said in a whisper.

"Yeah, weren't they pretty warlike? I suppose they had to be, what with everyone invading England. Devon! Please tell me you're going to stay in England longer than just a few days."

We moved over to join the chat with Devon and Fang, but after ten minutes of general catching up, everyone broke for their rooms to get ready for the parties.

"Hen party commences directly after lunch," I told everyone as they all dispersed into various rooms on the second and third floors. "Fang's bachelor do will happen when Brother rolls in. Just remember, Devon—"

"No sex workers, I know," he said with a flash of a grin almost as nice as Fang's.

"I don't care who you have at the party," I said, surprised he thought I'd doubt the man of my dreams. "I just don't want you to get him in a fight like you have the last three times you had stag dos."

"I've told you that after my last marriage, I'm off weddings," Devon said, holding up his hands, but with a wicked glint in his eyes. "There's only one woman who could change my mind, and alas, she's marrying my best mate."

I looked heavenward for a few seconds. "If you even think about asking me if I remember—"

"Hey, you remember the time when you were my girlfriend for the summer?" Devon interrupted, leaning casually against his open room door, trying hard not to grin. "How many times did you kiss me?"

"It was a month, and most of that time I was in Paris," I said with one of Mom's dramatic sighs, and looked at Fang. "How about Brother as your best man?"

Fang laughed, gave Devon a friendly bro-punch to the arm, then bent me backward in a steamy kiss. "Is that romantic enough?" he asked me.

"Enough to make my knees weak," I said, fanning myself.

Devon applauded, then gave me a perfectly platonic kiss on the cheek before pulling Fang into a hug. "Don't bother giving me a death glare, Emily. I knew the minute you laid eyes on Fang that I'd never have a shot. You are the only two people who I believe were truly meant for each other."

"Damn straight. Lunch is in half an hour. My hen party will be mostly at the spa next door, although Mace said we can use the bar if we want. There's no formal dinner planned, but Mace will have some sandwiches and things for us to nibble on if we get back from the parties and have the munchies." I gave Devon another swift hug, then tugged Fang after me as we headed down the back stairs to the kitchen.

"I thought everything was set for tomorrow?" Fang asked as we emerged into a small kitchen area at the back of the building.

"It was, but Mace texted me a few minutes ago that he needs to check in with us. And there is the man himself," I said when Mace and three people in dark clothes turned to look at us.

"Ah, there you are. Yes, yes, just so. This … erm … this is …" He eminded me of a goldfish what with his mouth opening and closing a few times.

"I'm Janice. We're here to help out with your wedding," the woman in front said, and whipped out a white server's apron. "Mr. Abbot hired us especially for the event. And now, we should really start getting things ready, yes?"

She asked the last of Mace, who nodded quickly. "Yes, absolutely. Prepare. Good idea. Erm … Emily, Fang, might I have a word in your ears? Just for a moment."

"Is something wrong?" Fang asked, moving with me so as to let the three helpers out. "Our ceremony is pretty simple, so we were under the impression that everything was set."

"Set, yes, everything is set," Mace said, nodding again. "There's no problem with the wedding or reception, but tonight … I assure you, nothing is going to affect your night's sleep. Nothing at all. It's just a few extra people, and I swear they will not get in your way. In fact, you probably won't even know they're here."

"Are you talking about Amy and Corbin Monroe? Because they are part of the party—" I started to say, but Mace, with a glance back into the kitchen, shooed us out to the reception area, which was now empty.

"I assure you, *assure* you, there is nothing to worry about. Everything is under control. The slight, unimportant change won't bother you or your guests at all."

"You don't have any food?" I guessed. "The bakery called and said a dog ate the cake before they delivered it? The officiant has given up marrying people, and run off to Brazil? I sure hope not, because it took a minor miracle to book her for the wedding. She's got a huge Instagram following, and is very in demand for weddings, so if she's not able to make the ceremony—"

"No, no, nothing at all like that," he said in a near whisper, looking scandalized. He glanced toward the door that led to the kitchen. "It's just that Gerard got a little confused, just slightly confused, about the dates, and booked a prestigious ghost-hunting group into the hotel for the night to investigate our upper stories."

"Ghosts? I didn't know this place was haunted. Did you know?" I asked Fang.

"No. What will these ghost hunters be doing?" he asked Mace, a single crease wrinkling the space between his brows. "As you know, both the hen and stag parties will keep most of us out for a few hours, but we will be back for a late supper."

"Do not panic," Mace said, holding up a hand and speaking in what I'm sure was his best authoritarian tone. "We've already booked the Spirited Lives people—they have a YouTube channel, evidently—into the Bide-a-Wee B&B just down the road, so they won't be a bother at all."

"So long as people don't go into our rooms, I don't care if they poke around the building," I said slowly. I was mildly annoyed, but decided that in the big picture, it didn't matter if there were a few extra people hanging around the hotel.

Fang leaned close and whispered into my ear, "They'll be damned lucky if your mother doesn't rope the whole group into attending the ceremony tomorrow."

I had to turn my laugh into a cough, so as not to offend Mace.

"Of course, of course, and I'm sure you'll have a delightful time with your respective parties," Mace reassured us, but his voice dropped when he glanced over his shoulder. "Don't think too harshly of Gerard, I beg you. He truly thought you were coming in tomorrow, and that the hotel would be completely empty tonight. As it is, he has spoken to the leaders, and they understand that they are not allowed into any guest rooms, and will confine themselves to the attic areas."

"Doesn't sound like it will be a problem, then," Fang said in his calm, reassuring-animals voice.

"I'd rather have a few ghost people around than no cake," I told him, thinking about the delicious chocolate orange wedding cake a local bakery was making for us. "I have plans to take home the leftovers, since everyone knows calories don't count for a bride on her day."

"You plan to eat *all* the leftovers in the space of a day?" Fang asked as Mace hurried off into the back rooms, and we started up the stairs.

"I'm stretching 'day' to mean three or four days. Depending on how much cake is left. I'll save you a piece," I offered.

"You are munificence personified," he said, and I could feel him reaching to pinch my butt when the entrance door opened with a gust of wind that sent a ripple through the rack of tourist pamphlets.

"Whew! No wonder there were so many ship-wrecks on this coast. That wind is wild—Emily!"

"Oh, good, you did get here," I said, tugging Fang with me when I did a one-eighty and headed down the stairs to greet the newcomers. "I wondered if you would change your mind. This is Fang Baxter, love of my life and vet extraordinaire."

Amy congratulated Fang, introduced her husband—who had nice eyes and an infectious smile—and then tried to apologize. "We got in yesterday, as a matter of fact. I'm still a bit torn about being here and intruding on your special day—"

"Eh," I said, leaning into Fang. "I told you before it doesn't really matter. And actually …" I glanced at Fang.

He raised his eyebrows at me, clearly letting me make the decision.

Never being one to waste time, I said quickly, "Actually, I was wondering if you had hired someone for the job? The one I interviewed for, that is."

"No, we haven't," Corbin said slowly, sliding Amy a questioning look. She slid it right back to him; then they both considered us. "We haven't been impressed by any of the other applicants. Did you have someone to recommend, or perhaps you've changed your mind?"

"More the latter, but … perhaps we could talk about it after tomorrow? If you're still going to be here, that is."

Amy's expression lightened. "We will, and I'm delighted to know circumstances have changed. I know you will fit in perfectly with the rest of the team, and—"

"My love, let us give the happy couple a little space before we have to sit down and negotiate," Corbin said with a chuckle, his arms around Amy.

"I'm so sorry," Amy said instantly, looking embarrassed. "I got a bit carried away with excitement. It's been a grueling few weeks, and this is our second day of actual vacation, so I'm finding it a bit hard to slip back into relaxation mode."

Something occurred to me then. I eyed Amy.

"Er …" she said in response to the eyeing.

"My hen party—bachelorette party—is going to start in about twenty minutes. I'd love it if you joined us. It's just my mother, aunt, bestie, and her wife. My teen cousin has opted to go with the men on some sort of zombie thing that will make up the stag do, but the rest of us are going to the spa next door for facials and hot stone massages and herbal hair treatments, and even a mud detox thing that I'm sure is going to be unpleasant, because who wants to sit in mud full of other people's toxins? But you don't have to mud up if you don't want to."

"Mud up?" Amy asked, then smiled. "That is so sweet of you, Emily, but I would feel very much like I was intruding—"

"Well, don't," I told her. "I'm sorry to sound blunt, but as I've said, our wedding is a very casual, having-a-good-time situation. I'd be happy to have you join the rest of us in the spa, but I would never want to put you on the spot, so if you'd prefer to not join us, that's fine, too."

"But Corbin—" she started to protest.

"Can join me and come to the stag do, if he likes," Fang offered.

I beamed at him. He was the most perfect man in the world, even if he did hog the covers, liked raisins, and fell asleep during episodes of *Naked and Afraid*.

"Now, that really would be intruding," Corbin said. "At least Amy and Emily have met, and have some sort of a relationship."

"Like Emily said, eh." Fang held out his hand and shook Corbin's. "Now we're acquainted, so you are welcome to come with us if you like, although I warn you it's not going to be a standard lads' night out. Emily's father, uncle, and niece are joining us, as well as one of my mates. That's it."

"There won't be any strippers, because my niece is only fourteen," I told them. "Most importantly, there won't be any fighting. I explicitly told Devon—that's Fang's best man—that there was to be no fighting like there was on all of his previous stag dos. So, you'd be perfectly safe there."

The next ten minutes was spent in discussion, but in the end, Amy and Corbin went off to their room to get ready for the parties, while Fang and I did the same.

"I will see you later, my darling," I told him, kissing him all over his handsome face. "Supple, coated with oils and unguents, and possibly toxin-laden mud in locations, but filled with love for you."

"I look forward to locating all the bits of mud clinging to you, my silky-skinned vixen," he said in his best serial-villain impression. "I will have no mercy in cleansing you of it."

"Oooh," I said with a little shimmy against him, backing off when Holly tapped on the door and said everyone was waiting. "I'll hold you to that. Let me know if Brother does something embarrassing. I'm collecting anecdotes to include in my second autobiography."

He laughed, and glanced at his watch. "Devon is holding back the start, but if your dad missed his train, we might have to leave without him."

"That's OK," I told him, opening the door. "I warned him he might have to make his way out to you if his tour du jour was late ending. Yes, I'm ready to go, Holly. Happy stag night, soon-to-be husband."

"Have fun with your hen party," he responded, shooing me out the door. "Just don't do anything that your father can hold over your head for years to come."

It's almost like he could see into the future.

SIX
THE ENSEMBLE

SUPERINTENDENT JANICE TOLE, COMMANDER: Hotel Lobby
17 August

"This report concerns the investigation of Supplemental Case number 433 on 17 August at the Foxglove and Nightshade Inn located in St. Gwynn." Superintendent Tole glanced up in irritation when Constable Harris burst into the small pantry, glancing around wildly for her. "Superintendent Tole is commanding the investigation, and—"

"There you are, ma'am. We have the cameras that you ordered, but unfortunately, their batteries are all dead."

Superintendent Tole glared at the constable, not only for interrupting her when she was recording a report to be typed up later by one of what she thought of as the "office flunkies," but mostly because she had told the team three days ago to make sure sufficient equipment was made available. "And now here we are with dead cameras," she continued her train of thought out loud.

"Yes?" the constable said, clearly unsure of the appropriate response.

Superintendent Tole fought the urge to demand the constable get up to speed, and instead told him, "Take them back to the station and get them charged. Yes, now. Right now. Sooner than now."

The constable's face scrunched up in a manner that reminded Superintendent Tole of a prune. "How can I do something sooner than now?"

"Just go! Get them charged!" she said louder than she intended, but managed to get him out the door so she could continue dictating her report. "Virtual and in-person surveillance and observation was conducted by three members of the Cornwall CID, consisting of Superintendent J. Tole, Inspector D. Walnes, and, regrettably, Constable J. J. Harris."

She was silent for a moment, then added, "Delete the word 'regrettably.' Continuing. On the date of 17 August, three members of the Spirited Lives group were witnessed arriving at 14:55. They were greeted by the hotel co-owner, Mr. Gerard Abbot, and shown upstairs to the fourth floor, which is made up of a series of four consecutive attic storage rooms. Two rooms were semifurnished in what co-owner Mr. Mace Abbot referred to as 'emergency hidey-holes to be used in case of a zombie apocalypse.' It is unclear whether or not Mr. Abbot believes society is threatened by fictional beings."

"Ma'am?" Inspector Walnes popped his head into the pantry, holding out his phone to show the superintendent. "I'm afraid we didn't get the search warrant, and since the hotel owners refuse to put up the cameras without it …"

Superintendent Tole tightened her lips against the scream she wanted to release. Why was it that the (in her opinion, ridiculously inept) hotel thieves somehow managed to thwart her every attempt to catch them in the act?

"Ma'am? Shall I tell Constable Harris to leave the cameras and return to duty?" the inspector asked, his eyes guarded.

She turned away, her fingers tight around the phone into which she was recording. It took her a minute to be able to speak without roaring at the injustices of not being able to record the comings and goings at the hotel. "Yes. Just … keep him out of my way."

"As you like," the inspector said before backing out of the pantry and quietly closing the door.

"Per instructions, the CID team has separated, with Superintendent Tole monitoring the basement kitchen and staff areas (Zone 2: Domestic Spaces), Inspector Walnes surveilling activity outside the hotel (Zone 1: Exterior), and Constable Harris monitoring comings and goings of all hotel guests and visitors (Zone 3: Guest and Public Rooms). Cameras would have eliminated the need for so many personnel to be deployed around the hotel on surveillance detail, but given the lack of support in that area, the team will conduct their investigation accordingly."

She bit off the urge to add, "And a fat lot of good it'll do when even if we do catch them red-handed, they'll be out within twenty-four hours."

She thought it, though. She thought it many, many times.

EMILY: The Spa

"So," I said, squirming a little to scoot the towel wrapped around me so that it was more comfy. "Here we all are, a bunch of married women and me. I assume a solid round of matronly advice is to be passed out."

"Bridal advice!" Kathie said, stretching out on the upper wooden plank of the sauna. "Sounds like fun. Ah, this heat is glorious. Sweat-inducing, but glorious. Really makes you feel like your pores are flowing freely."

"And now I have to visit the restroom," Mom said, getting up, but snagging a glass of champagne from Daisy, the spa owner, as she brought us beverages before checking the temperature was to our liking.

"Sorry," Kathie called after Mom toddled off. "I forgot you have a weak bladder."

"Kegels," Marla said, fanning herself with one hand, while accepting a flute of champagne with the other. "So good for the pelvic floor."

"We Kegel for five minutes a day, each morning while we're having our breakfast," Holly told me. "I don't know that it's doing any good, but I figure it can't hurt."

"They are supergood for you. My ob-gyn says every Kegel you do can mean not using one pair of old-lady bladder pants down the line," Kathie said, taking the glass Holly offered. "Now, this is what I call fun: sauna heat with ice-cold champagne."

"My mother—who we won't go into now, because she's got more issues than a periodical, and also because I just met all of you excepting for Emily—always scoffed at the idea of Kegels, and just look at where that landed her—with a bladder holder-upper device." Amy leaned against the wooden wall, her legs stretched out in front of her on the bench. I was glad to see she'd gotten over the worst of feeling awkward, and was now obviously relaxed and enjoying herself.

"A what, now?" I asked.

"Pessary," Mom said as she reentered the room, glass in hand. "Your grandma has one, Emily. It's why I taught you girls to do those hoo-haw exercises."

"Kegels," Amy, Holly, and Marla said with synchronized perfection.

"Right, so married-women advice number one: Kegel more. Gotcha." I sipped at my own beverage. I wasn't much of a drinker, but I did like champagne, and this one was particularly light and bubbly. "I promise I'll start a daily Kegel regime. What other bride advice do you guys have?"

The silence that followed my question was broken only by Mom absentmindedly ladling water onto the stones. The enveloping cloud of steam filled the small sauna.

"And that wraps up the 'advice to the bride' portion of the hen party," I said with a little giggle into my champagne glass.

"It's not that I wouldn't love to give you advice, but you've been living quite happily with Fang for fourteen years, and I don't think any suggestions I have are going to be better than what you two are doing. Together. Not sex, the other. Interactions," Mom said, waving her hand, which unfortunately was the one holding her champagne glass, spilling some of it onto her bare leg. "Whoops. I can't possibly be tiddly on half a glass of champers."

"One," I said, looking sternly at her as I handed her my spare towel, which I was covertly using to wipe up the under-boob sweat, "you most definitely are heading straight for snockered, and two, since when do you say the word 'champers'? That's wholly out of character."

"Your dad makes me watch his favorite British TV shows," she said, mopping up her leg before refilling her glass.

Holly and Marla had been whispering together, and as one, they turned to face me. Holly gave me a wry smile and said, "I hate to fail you if you really need advice, but I agree with your mother. You and Fang are so happy together. What could we suggest other than what you're doing?"

"Kegels aside," Marla said. Her expression changed to one of abstracted thought. "In fact, I'm going to do a minute or two of them now, since we all know how alcohol runs through you."

"Good idea. I wonder if I can do it lying down?" Kathie asked. "Hey, I can! This may open up new avenues of possibilities."

I looked around at the women in the sauna. Each and every one of them had that same look of distracted focus.

"You all look constipated," I told them. "Wait. Let me try. Someone tell me if I look like that, too."

"Oh, definitely," Kathie said, lifting her head to squint at me. "You look like you haven't pooped in a week."

I released the inner muscles and sighed. "Fine, I won't do it in front of Fang. We can spend the rest of our time in the sauna shooting the breeze, metaphorically speaking."

Lazy chat followed for a bit, Mom and Amy and Kathie talking about their lives back in the US, while Holly, Marla, and I gossiped like old ladies.

But it was when I caught something my aunt said that I leaned back to look at her.

"—doesn't want to sell, of course, but he's refusing to admit he doesn't recover from injury as fast as he used to."

"Is he not able to go out with the sheep?" Mom asked.

"His stamina isn't an issue—" Kathie made a face when both Mom and Amy giggled. We were on our third bottle of champagne by then, and everyone was feeling pretty relaxed and happy. "Yes, in that way, too, but walking the fields itself isn't the problem. It's all of it dumped on him. We could survive without the income the farm brings in, but I honestly don't think Iain could survive without the farm."

Everyone was listening now.

"Is something wrong with your uncle?" Holly asked softly.

"Bad leg, evidently," I answered. "He fell off a mountain."

"Ouch," she said in sympathy.

"I say sell the farm to Iain's son—the good one, what's his name?" Mom asked, getting caught in a couple of hiccups.

"David," Kathie said, sitting up now, and holding out her glass when Amy waggled the bottle at everyone.

"That's the one. Sell to him, move to a smaller spot where you can have a wee little house on a wee little farm with those adorable wee little animals." Mom nodded a couple of times, and set down her glass. "Hoo. I think I am now well and fully lubricated, so I'll stop."

"A small farm might work," Kathie said, her normally sunny expression fading. "But Iain loves our farm. He didn't mind hacking off a piece of it to go to David because one of his boys is already saying he wants to take over one day, but I don't know if I could get Iain to part with the remainder of the farm. I worry it would break his heart."

"The answer is simple, then," I said, pouring the last bit of champagne into my glass. I had kept my drinking to a minimum, since I wanted to enjoy my time with my friends and family.

"If it is, then I'd love to hear it," Kathie said. "Iain and I have been discussing options for several months, and we're no closer to finding a working solution than when he was laid up with his broken knee."

I set down my glass, and donned my best explainer voice. "I can tell you the answer in one word: tourists."

"How on earth would tourists help us?" Kathie asked.

"Remember when you got married?" I asked Kathie. "And we all came over to watch, and then Iain and his sons showed up in kilts, and all the women in our family went gaga? That's what you do."

"Get married for tourists?" Kathie asked, her face scrunched up.

"Provide men-in-kilts experiences for tourists. Americans, mostly, cause we're the craziest for that sort of thing. Make Iain's farm a Highland Sheep Glamping Experience. The tourists can stay in yurts that you set up in the fields, watch Clara make goat's milk soap, interact with the couple of pet sheep you guys keep, and go riding. You still have horses, right?"

"Yes," Kathie said, now looking at the wall of the sauna with an intensity that far outmatched her Kegel face. "Trail rides through the pastures, up onto the ridge. Picnic lunches. Maybe even a petting-zoo type situation for the kids." She suddenly stood up and pulled me into a bear hug. "Emily! That was a brilliant suggestion. I can't wait to tell Iain. Clara could have a little shop—she'd be thrilled by that."

"People could learn how to milk goats," Holly suggested.

"Maybe your daughter could teach them how to make soap, and they could make a bar of their own. I'd pay for that sort of a class," Marla said.

"Oh, me too!" I said at the same time that Mom, a lifelong learner, murmured something about needing such a class in her life.

"I have to get my phone," Kathie said, pulling open the sauna door, allowing cold air to swirl around us as she dashed out. "I have to make some notes so I can present them to Iain later on. He's going to be thrilled with the idea of staying on the farm, but making it far more reasonable as we get older. Brilliant! Absolutely brilliant!"

"Doesn't your step-daughter-in-law do catering?" I called after her, gathering up my towels as I slowly headed out of the sauna. "She could charge tourists for meals."

"Ack! She could!" Kathie screamed, diving into the curtained cubicle she'd been given to change. "Brilliant, brilliant, brilliant!"

"Well, at least we offered some good advice, even if it wasn't to you," Holly said as we all entered our respective changing spaces.

"We've definitely used our superpowers for good," I agreed, and went to shower before the massages.

CORBIN MONROE: Reception/Lounge

"Any word on Brother?"

Corbin, who was reading some email on his phone, glanced up when two men entered the small seating area in the reception. He recognized the speaker as a man named Devon, while the other was the oddly named groom.

"His train should be arriving in fifteen minutes," Fang answered, moving to the side when Iain, the dark-haired Scot, limped into the room. "I suppose one of us should fetch him, since getting a ride would probably take a while."

"I am not taking the party limo out to a train station," Devon told Fang. "It's too expensive, and besides, it's all set up for us, and I don't want everything messed about. But I would take your car."

"I can get him—" Fang started to say.

Devon pushed him into a chair. "You're the groom. Just sit here and be groomy. Give me your keys."

"I think it'd be best if I was to be getting Brother," Iain said, shooting a swift, assessing look toward Devon. "As you've been having a few already."

"You're a guest—" Fang protested, but was immediately shut down.

"He's my brother-in-law. Kathie wouldn't care if I didn't fetch him, but I've got the MacLaren honor to represent," Iain said with a wink as he left.

"He has a point," Devon said, then sat on the sofa next to Corbin, giving him a curious once-over.

Corbin returned the gesture, then shifted his attention to Fang, trying to assess whether the young man had asked him along to his bachelor party in hopes of scoring points on his wife's behalf.

"Emily told Amy that she was a big gamer," he said in a subtle attempt to see if he was going to be waylaid by attempts to sway his opinion on Emily. "Do you play, too?"

"Some," Fang said, propping his feet up on a hideous, squat ottoman. "Emily's much better at most games than I am. I tend to lean toward puzzles, whereas she likes immersive games. Elves and warlocks and things like that."

"I'm the same," Corbin said, wary. "I'll tell you a secret—even though I'm the game creator, I'm far from the most proficient player."

Neither man said anything, just looked mildly interested.

Devon pulled out his phone.

"So, Emily's abilities would be valuable," Corbin ended lamely. He almost flinched the minute the words came out. He couldn't remember when he'd been so awkward and brazen with a fishing attempt.

"I know she's anxious to talk to you and Amy after the wedding," Fang said, then consulted his phone when it pinged at him. "Emily says the ladies have had a breakthrough. I wonder what sort of breakthrough, and whether it involves actual breakage."

Devon snorted a laugh.

Corbin raised an eyebrow. "Does she normally break things?"

"Emily?" Fang thought for a moment. "Not intentionally, no. But things happen around her."

"You can say that again," Devon muttered, his gaze still on his phone. "She attracts chaos like chum attracts sharks."

"Sometimes," Fang allowed. "But a lot of times, crazy just seems to find her. She never goes looking for it."

"Speaking of her sister, is she going to be here for the ceremony?" Devon asked.

"Supposedly," Fang said with a brief casting of his eyes skyward.

Corbin wondered if Amy was so sure about Emily being a good candidate, and took a minute to text

Amy to ask if she was having a good time with the bride's party before resigning himself to spending an evening with a bunch of new acquaintances.

The two younger men talked for a few minutes before Fang asked, "Why did you book a limo, anyway? There's not that many of us."

"Ah, but we're going to have fun on the way to the venue," Devon said.

"You remember that Clara will be with us," Fang warned.

"I remember." He grinned. "She'll love it. It's all prep for the venue. You want to see? It won't spoil anything."

Devon leaped up and Fang, with a wry smile at Corbin, followed him outside.

"Alone again," Corbin said to the empty room, and resumed reading emails.

A door to what he assumed was the office swung open just enough for a man in his midthirties to poke his head into the room. He stared at Corbin.

Corbin stared back.

"You here for the wedding?" the man asked. He was British, and obviously one of the wedding party.

"Emily's wedding? More or less," Corbin said, not wanting to appear like he was a family friend.

The man nodded. "We'll be back later, when the heat is off. But keep your eye out. We need all the help we can get."

Corbin didn't have the slightest idea how to respond, but the point was moot, because as soon as the man finished speaking, he withdrew his head and quietly closed the door.

"Well, that was odd." He thought for a moment, then decided it was nothing to do with him, and returned to dealing with business.

FANG BAXTER: Garden

"I'm worried."

"Eh." Devon, who had strolled around the hotel to the minuscule back garden, leaned on a waist-high fence and looked out into sunlit hills. "It's just cold feet. We all get them. It'll be OK once the wedding is over. Until then, just remind yourself that if it wasn't for Emily, you'd end up marrying someone good for you."

It took Fang a moment to work through the sentence, mostly because Devon had insisted on toasting the bride with a few nips of whiskey, and although Fang wasn't close to inebriated, he could feel his normal level of reserve had melted away into nothing. "Actually, I'm not worried about marrying Em at all. She may not be perfect, but we suit each other. I'm worried that she's going to regret not having her father here for the actual ceremony."

"Now, that is a valid concern," Devon said, plopping down at a white metal table, and pulling out a flask.

He offered it to Fang, who shook his head. He was as fond of a stag-do buzz as the next man, but he felt a bit more responsibility in the role of groom.

"Have you talked about it at all with her?" Devon continued.

Fang slowly pulled out a second chair and moved

it into the shade before sitting. "Yes. And she insists that it's what she wants."

"It can't be that she's avoiding your question, because Emily always says everything she's thinking, so either she's lying or you're worrying unduly. I'd say it's the latter."

It was on the tip of Fang's tongue to tell his oldest friend that Emily had matured during the last sixteen years, but decided it wasn't important at that moment. "I love the fact that she tells me everything, to be honest. I never have liked people who put on masks to go along with what they think you want. I may never know what Emily is going to say, but I do know that what it is will be truthful."

Devon, still holding the flask, pointed at him. "You're ripped, mate. You'd never let that sort of grammar by if you were sober."

"Slightly ripped," Fang corrected. "And since I want to enjoy the stag do, I think I'll pass on any more right now, thanks."

"Smart. I'm not nearly so sage," Devon said, and took another swig. "So if it's not the thing with Brother—no, wait, Emily said he's going by a nom de plume for this trip. What's his name?"

Fang felt a sigh rise up. "Detective Inspector Mortimer. I think. Something like that."

Just as he was speaking, a van pulled into the delivery lot, and three men emerged. Fang didn't pay them much mind, assuming they were bringing supplies for the wedding and meals.

"Right, so if it's not DI Mortimer being on the trail of … what, notorious jewel thieves? … thus missing your wedding, then what is really causing you to look a good ten years older than normal?"

"Christ," Fang said, running a hand through his hair. "I had no idea I look like hell. Emily told me this morning that my bare chest—never mind. I just wish Henry—Detective Inspector Mortimer—would get here in time, but I guess I'm going to have to let it go. He'll get here when he gets here."

The first of the men from the van was staggering in with a large black bin but paused when Fang spoke, and shot him a wild look before turning to face the van. The man was dressed in black cargo trousers patterned with hot pink turtles. Or lizards. Or perhaps dinosaurs. Fang eyed him for few seconds, wondering if he was planning on wearing the same trousers at the reception dinner.

"It's going to be hell having the ole inspector for a father-in-law, you know," Devon said, leaning back in his chair, gazing out at the hilly fields that rolled back from the town.

The man with the turtle trousers scurried back to the van, still holding his bin.

"I don't see why," Fang said after several moments' thought. His brain felt a little slow, like it was floating in molasses. He definitely needed to stay away from Devon's flask. "Henry and I took each other's number many years ago. We get along pretty well, although he does tend to get a bit bossy telling me that I'm far too young to think of fatherhood."

Two of the other van men slid around the back of the vehicle, and stood with their heads close together as they faced the hotel.

"But you and Em don't want kids," Devon said, shooting him a questioning look.

"That's right, and we've told her parents several times. I don't think they object, per se."

The third man handed the heavy bin to one of the other men, who strode forward purposely, slowing down as he passed Fang.

"Then what?" Devon asked.

Fang shrugged. "I think Hen—DI Mortimer is simply worried that Emily or Bess will give way to their respective biological clocks before he can brace himself to the idea of being a grandfather. It's all speculation, but it's the only thing we can think of."

"You can ask him when he gets here." Devon frowned at his phone. "I hope your uncle isn't going to take long fetching him. The Boot Camp place is very popular, and although we're booked for the whole night, I don't want them getting ideas about giving away our slot. You sure your niece will like it?"

Fang noticed from the corner of his eye that the man with the bin finally reached the hotel, whereupon he turned around and stared at his companions for a good half minute before entering door to the kitchen. "You haven't seen her since she was, what, four or five? She's smart as a whip, and very focused. She'll love the whole idea of being a survivor in the zombie apocalypse."

"Ahem," Devon said, pulling out his phone. "What I have reserved for your enjoyment is nothing quite so lame. Where is the … ah. Here we go."

One of the remaining van men bolted up the narrow gravel path to the hotel. He carried a gray bag.

Fang's phone pinged. He read the message. "Iain says he has the detective inspector, and they are on their way back. Should be here in a few."

"Good. We'll have to get going in the next fifteen minutes or we'll miss the wing buffet. Let's see. … *Darkness creeps, and in its depths, death lurks in the form of a horde of maniacal zombies. Your mission is to negotiate the corridors of our specially built facility, dodging smoke, stairways, rubble, and dark rooms. In your race against the clock, you'll test your wits—and the aim of your laser rifle—against the horde of zombies who seem to know every move you take.* Tell me that doesn't sound like fun!"

"It'll be a lot of fun, Dev; you can stop worrying we won't like it."

"I'm not worrying about you," Devon said, idly watching as the third van guy strolled past them with studied nonchalance. He carried the type of padded bag frequently used by cameramen. "It's the inspector who concerns me. And now evidently your uncle broke his knee. Luckily, I had the Boot Camp place do the less activity, more escape-room-ish setup, since I wanted to keep it reasonable for your niece."

"That girl can probably run faster, farther, and longer than both of us. Combined," Fang said, mildly startled when all three men burst from the hotel and hurried past them to the van. His phone burbled again. "Good. Iain and the inspector are here. Shall we?"

As they rose and turned toward the hotel, Fang saw the face of one of the servers peering out of the window briefly before she seemed to melt into the dark interior.

A thought flitted so quickly through his brain that he almost didn't register it: where Emily went, chaos inevitably followed.

He dismissed it along with the ever-present worry about whether the move to the US was smart, if he'd have trouble finding a job, and how difficult it would be fitting in. "Let the stag do commence."

"Amen and fuck yeah," Devon responded, following him into the hotel.

Fang dismissed the single twinge of concern about the oddness of the hotel employees. It was all bound to be nothing.

EMILY: Guest Rooms

Tap.
I paused in the act of brushing my hair.
Tap.
I stared at the radiator, but it was now silent.
I returned to awkwardly angling my head down enough to see it in the mirror that had, due to the eaves, been set at roughly belly-button height.
Tip. Tap.
"OK, what the hell is going on here?" I asked, straightening up to look around the room. "Is this place really haunted? If so, kindly go to another room to wait for the ghost dudes."

A flash of white at the window caught my eye as I was bent over trying to tame my hair.

"Bess?" I hurried to the window and fought with the stiff Victorian latch to swing it open. "What on earth … are you in a tree?"

"Yes, and it's damned uncomfortable. Here, take Herbert."

"Are you insane?" I grabbed the plastic pet carrier that barely fit through the window. "Who or what is a Herbert? And why are you in a tree?"

"Who has time for questions?" my sister asked, and, to my shock, started climbing down the tree.

"Bess, wait!" I yelled, leaning out of the window.

"Shush," she cautioned, but paused her descent. "What's wrong?"

"Let's start with who Herbert is, and then move on to why you're in a tree instead of walking in the door like a normal person."

She gave an audible sigh.

"I told you about the cockfighting people. Herbert is one of the birds."

I stared at the pet carrier, now sitting on the floor. I couldn't see inside it. "You gave me a rooster named Herbert? Is he a wedding present?"

"He's a pigeon, not a rooster. They all are, as it turns out. We rescued three—Herbert, Louie, and Patrice. Herbert will be fine with you because Fang will make sure he's not sick. We may or may not be at the dinner tonight. It depends if Monk has found where Patrice flew off to when we were rescuing them."

"But ... that doesn't explain why you couldn't just come into the hotel."

"Are you kidding?" Bess shot me a look dripping with annoyance. "I heard someone talking into a radio out in the car park, and knew it had to be the cops looking for us. The bird-fighting organization clearly has the local police in their back pocket, and sent them here to nab Monk and me. We only *just* got released for the damage we did to that fur-processing plant in Sussex, and I simply do not have time to go back to jail again. Not now. Take care of Herbert."

I have to admit that my wits weren't any too hot, because I just stared blankly as my sister continued her way down the big oak next to the hotel and disappeared into the growing shadows.

"A pigeon. My sister has stolen a fighting pigeon, and given him to me. Even Mom isn't going to be able to excuse this sort of behavior. Well, let's just see what sort of shape you're in. I hope you're not hurt, because Fang is off at his bachelor shindig … awww."

While I was speaking, I'd unlatched the wire front of the carrier, and peered inside. A small bowl of water was attached to the interior of the carrier, along with a thick pale-blue towel, on top of which sat a gray pigeon, perfectly normal in appearance … except for the cowboy outfit he wore, complete with a cowboy hat held on with a little strap, fringed chaps, and a faux leather vest with bandolier.

The pigeon emerged from the carrier and looked around with bright, shiny black eyes. I held out my hand, and to my surprise, he hopped onto it, pausing to preen a shoulder before turning back to give me the once-over.

"OK, you are far cuter than I imagined, although the outfit looks uncomfortable. Shall we take it off?"

A knock sounded at the door just as I gently poked at the hat to see if the evil bird people had done something to it, but it slid right off.

I rose, and carried Herbert to the door.

"Miss Emily, someone left a package for you at the front desk—oh." Mace blinked a couple of times at Herbert. The bird did the same, tipping his head to the side to consider Mace better. I half-hoped Mace would do the same, but he just stared at us both. "You have a bird."

"I didn't have one when I came in," I pointed out. "My sister just gave him to me. He's a wedding present, and his name is Herbert. Is that birdseed? Thank god. I was going to have to text Bess that I had no idea what a pigeon ate."

"Is there a reason why he is in a costume?" Mace said after handing over a plastic bag filled with a variety of bird food, nutrients, and even a couple of toys.

My sister may be a few raisins short of a fruitcake, but she would lay her life on the line to save needy animals. It's one of the reasons why she respects Fang so much.

"Whimsy?" I asked as I gently closed the door. It was a bit drafty in the hallway, and although it had been a balmy day, it was too windy for my liking. "Right. Let's get you sorted. But first, let's get your aunts in here to see you."

Holly responded to my text demanding her presence in a few minutes, and entered the room only to stop and stare. "Is that … Emily, do you have … it's a cowboy?"

"His name is Herbert, and he's hungry. Once he's done snacking on his pellets and seeds, I have a couple of berries for him. Or rather, Bess included some berries and greens. And yes, I'm going to take off the rest of his outfit once he's done dining. He has a little hat, but I took it off, because who wants to eat while a hat is bobbing around on your head?"

"Emily, I—" Holly stopped, shook her head, then tapped on her phone, saying into it, "She has a pigeon named Herbert. He's a cowboy. No, her sister, evidently. All right." She ended the call, and knelt at where Herbert was dining out of a small bowl. "Marla is coming. She's never seen a cowboy pigeon before. Why did Bess—"

"It's Bess," I said as an answer, then told Marla to come in when she knocked. "Do you have to ask anything more?"

"He *is* a cowboy!" Marla was delighted, and immediately sat cross-legged on the floor. True to form, Herbert, who had been standing next to me while he ate, stopped, took one look at Marla (a fellow animal person like Fang), and toddled over to her, pecking a couple of times at the hem of her jeans before he hopped onto her leg and squatted down, wiggling his butt as he got comfy. "And now I'm in love."

"We can't have him," Holly said quickly, a bit too quickly, but I knew from past discussions with Holly that Marla—like me—was a sucker for any animal, and she had to put down a foot on the number of animals they rescued.

"She's so mean," I told Marla, running a finger down Herbert's sleek head. He blinked a couple of times, then settled into himself like he was a big puffball, his eyes closing slowly. "Fang told me if I had my way, I'd have enough animals to open a zoo. They just don't understand us."

"I think they understand us far too well," Marla said, laughing. She and Holly exchanged adoring glances, and I felt all warm and fuzzy knowing that my bestie was loved and happy. "Stop sending me eyebrow semaphore, Holly. I'm not going to take him home. For one, he's Emily's. And for another, the cats would go crazy having him in the house. What are you going to tell Fang? I thought you guys had a two-pet limit?"

"Herbert is a wedding present," I said, carefully scooping Herbert up since he seemed to want to sleep, and peeling off the cowboy outfit before tucking him back into the carrier. I had torn up a bunch of newspaper, and set it in the back on top of a thick pad of the Sunday edition for Herbert to use as a litter box. Before closing his door, I set the bowl of pellets and seeds into the crate with him. He snuggled into the towel and looked sleepy. "Fang can't refuse to take a wedding present."

I wasn't so sure about that last point, but figured I'd worry about that later.

We spent another few minutes watching Herbert go to sleep before Marla said she wanted a nap before dinner. "The massage made me feel like a soggy noodle, and I swear it helped my cold," she said, stretching. "We have to get some of those stones, Holly. I could have lain there for hours while the masseuse covered me in stones."

"It was good," I agreed, getting to my feet. "Are you sure you're not up to the fire lessons? Dinner is at seven, but we should be through with the fire by six. I figured we'd want some time to recover."

"I think a nap would do me more good," she said, then headed off toward her room.

"I tried to pick things that I thought everyone would like," I said slowly, worried that Marla wasn't having as much fun as I'd hoped. "Does she have something against learning how to breathe fire? The lady who will be teaching us said it's perfectly safe to learn."

"No, she doesn't have a problem with it per se," Holly said in a choked voice. "It's just … oh, Emily. You are so uniquely you. Never, ever change." She came in for another bear hug, then trotted off to join Marla.

"Yeah, but unique in a good way, right?" I asked, leaning out of the doorway to yell after her. "Not like Bess? Right? *Right?*"

Laughter trailed after her as she turned the corner to her end of the hotel.

I thought of texting Fang that we had an addition to the family, but decided that discussion would be better kept until he was back from his stag do. Instead, I followed the lead of the others (Mom, Kathie, and Amy all said the massages and mud baths left them in need of a nap) and curled up on the bed, my phone open to a website on the care of pet pigeons.

Two hours later I emerged wearing an old tee and long pants, as requested by the fire-breathing teacher. As I headed for the back staircase, which split to head upward into the attic rooms, as well as leading down into a small room that opened to the garden, voices drifted down from on high.

"We'll have to grab him," a man's voice said. It was pitched low, but he must have been standing at the top of the stairs, because the noise echoed down the staircase to me.

"It's too dangerous," a second man's voice answered. He was more hushed, but by holding my breath and eavesdropping like crazy, I could just discern what he was saying. "We can't risk taking him. Someone would notice."

"Holy shit," I whispered under my breath, goose bumps breaking out on my arms. It was Bess's evil bird group! She was wrong about the people being police, but they definitely were there looking for Herbert.

"We can't risk *not* taking him," the first man said in a decisive voice, and footsteps sounded on the wooden stairs.

I hustled back into my room, double-checked that Herbert was fine, and then hauled him over to Holly's room.

"It's just until we're done breathing fire," I told Marla, who was snuggled into bed with a book and a pot of tea. "Then I'll pick him back up. Don't let anyone into the room who you don't know. Those evil bird peeps could be anywhere."

"I will protect Herbert with my life," Marla swore, and Holly and I left them to go out and get fiery.

TURTLE-TROUSER MAN: Attic

"Leon!"

"Will you shut it? Someone is going to hear you!"

Leon spun around to glare at Monty, who took a step back in response, causing him to brush against a dusty armoire.

He leaped forward and immediately dusted his lucky pair of turtle trousers. He wanted to protest Leon's tendency to be unreasonably snappish, not to mention cavalier in regard to his special trousers, but a lifetime experience of his cousin had him biting back the words. "Sorry. I thought I'd tell you since Ben left us here alone. Is he going to be back soon?"

"He's off dealing with his ex-wife, and will be back when he's back. Stop being such a baby about doing the job by ourselves. We'll be fine so long as you do as you're told. Did you find him?" Leon brushed past Monty to go into the second of the three attic rooms. This one was filled with the empty equipment containers that Leon insisted made them look legit.

Monty resisted the urge to twitch his shoulders in irritation. He hated it when Leon snapped at him. "The copper? He's nowhere."

"Are you daft? He has to be somewhere. We saw him roll in." Leon turned angry eyes on Monty. "You said you were going to be good on this job. I'm vouching for you. You'd better get your shit together, and do what I tell you to do."

"I am," Monty protested, feeling Leon was being overly critical of his participation. He had an unreasonable urge to tell his mum that once again Leon was bullying him. She always offered him solidarity against his dad's family. "I'm doing everything you say to do. I can't help it if he's not in the hotel."

"You can, because he's got to be here. They all are here. That waiter with the tits said there's a dinner in an hour. Now get back out there and find him. And if no one is around, nab him."

"What am I supposed to do to him?" Monty's voice echoed slightly, causing Leon to shush him and hurriedly close the door to the attic landing. "I can't haul him all around the place! You call me daft, but that plan is dafter than the daftiest daft thing."

"You're a real wanker, you know that? Here I bring you into the group, vouching for you to everyone, and we get sent here on this little job, and you're all up in my tits about doing your fair bit." Leon almost snarled when he spoke, making Monty once again take a step backward. "You bring him up here, OK? Can you stuff that in the thick sludge you call your head? Bring him up here."

"And then what?" Monty asked, bristling. He wanted badly to tell his cousin where he could stuff his stupid group, but decided to tell him off later, after they were done and had been paid. Then he'd tell Leon exactly what he thought. "Someone'll hear him."

"Not if he's tied up. We'll stuff him ..." Leon glanced around the obviously disused, dusty room with a sneer that Monty always dreaded. "In the back room, there. They have a big cupboard, big enough to hold him. Is that enough information for you, Mr. Nosy?"

"I like to have all the facts beforehand," was all Monty allowed himself to say before leaving the room, his dignity wrapped around him like a blanket.

He was very much looking forward to giving Leon an earful. He might even video it, so he could share it with his mum. She'd enjoy that almost as much as he would.

MACE ABBOT: Kitchen

Gerard peeked through the door to the dining room, and said softly, "Well, at least the ghost people aren't getting in the way of the wedding party."

"I should hope not! After all the trouble we went through getting everything settled." Mace, holding a basket of rolls, peeked alongside him. He counted heads. "We're missing two … oh, no, there they are."

"Everyone rest easy, Chief Detective Inspector Mortimer is here," the father of the bride announced as he entered the room. He sounded a bit liquid in his vowels, which had Mace narrowing his eyes on the man. He had a dislike of rowdy drunkards, but hadn't had to worry about that with this group … until now.

"Did you get a promotion?" the bride asked, but only after she stopped making sheep's eyes at the groom. "Weren't you just regular 'Detective Inspector' before?"

"It's in the pipeline," the father said, dismissing it as he made his way to the buffet. "Just as soon as my team and I solve the mystery of Redheads Inc. and their wave of country house crime. Ooh. Is that local fish? Chris, did you see the fish?"

A middle-aged woman with short blond hair, and who bore a variety of Celtic jewelry hung around her neck and both arms, lifted the lid on the pulled pork and breathed in appreciably. "I'm standing next to you, Brother. I can see the fish, but this pork smells divine."

"You like fish," he told her just as if he was having a moment of insight.

"Yes. And you're slightly drunk. Did you boys stop off at a pub after your zombie fun, by any chance?" the mother of the bride asked the room in general.

The men all cheered. "Two pubs, actually. The first got too rowdy, considering Emily refused to let us fight," a dark-haired man said. He, also, had a liquidity to his voice that had Mace making a mental note to keep a closer eye on the room than he might otherwise.

"Is the father police?" Gerard asked after glancing behind them to make sure the kitchen was empty of policemen.

"No. He's a professor of some sort," Mace whispered back. "The bride said he's on some mystery puzzle tour, and they adopt personas. That's his character name."

"How odd. Is he—" Gerard stopped as the bride and groom strolled past the barely open door toward the food dishes.

"—can't expect to move an aggressive pigeon with us to the States. They're bound to have laws, Em."

"We can take the animals," the bride pointed out, frowning. "Why would they allow us to take a dog and cat, but not a pigeon? And you haven't met Herbert. He's not aggressive. Oooh, lemon tarts!"

Gerard allowed the door to slowly close.

"An interesting couple, that," Mace said, approving of them on the whole. "The groom's a vet, you know. And she's some sort of scientist."

"Younger people have more education these days than we had," Gerard said, glancing at the clock. "I wonder if I should offer Mr. Adam some refreshments before they start their hunting. It's bound to be dusty in the attics. I think I'll just pop upstairs and see if they need anything."

Before Mace could answer that the ghost group would probably welcome being left on their own, the female detective suddenly appeared in the door to the cellars. "You leave them alone. Focus on your customers, as we requested."

"Absolutely," Mace said, giving Gerard's hand a supportive squeeze. "We understand the situation perfectly. We won't approach them unless they're on the ground floor."

She frowned. "You don't need to talk to them at all, no matter where they are."

"Madam, you asked us to act naturally while your team was present," Gerard said, causing Mace to glance at him in surprise. Gerard tended to be nonconfrontational, but his tone was decisive. "If a customer, even one who is poking around the attics looking for ghosts, is in one of this hotel's many public spaces, we will always interact with them. It is our duty as hosts to ensure our guests feel welcomed and valued."

Mace wanted to applaud, but confined himself to an even more supportive squeeze, breathing a sigh of relief when the superintendent, with an unladylike snort, snatched the basket of rolls from his hand and shoved past them to enter the dining room with a muttered, "Just see to it you stay out of our way."

"I can't wait for that to be gone," Gerard said with a whisper and a head nod toward the dining room. "I swear I'm as jumpy as a hedgehog on a roundabout with them underfoot."

"It'll be over tomorrow," Mace said, and wondered if it was wrong to want to lock Gerard and himself into their rooms and refuse to deal with anyone or anything for the next twenty-four hours.

As an escape, it sounded fabulous.

The superintendent stormed into the kitchen. "They want another bottle of champagne," she said with a toss of her head, then proceeded out to the garden, no doubt to camp inside the van they had tucked around the far side of the spa.

"Merde!" Gerard, who had gone to one of the two refrigerators to get the champagne, turned a stricken face toward Mace. "I forgot to pick up the salmon! It has to marinade overnight, and should be soaking now. I'll run to the shop and pray they still have it. Merde, merde, merde!"

As Gerard snatched up his car keys and dashed out of the kitchen, one of the police team poked his head into the kitchen to announce, "Your downstairs loo is broken. It won't stop running."

Mace slumped for a few seconds before squaring his shoulders. "So much for escape. Onward!"

SEVEN
SERIOUSLY???

EMILY
August 17th

"Wedding eve is closing not with a bang, but a whimper," I told my mother.

Holly and Marla tittered at the unintentional double entendre.

"Focus, ladies," I told them, glancing over my shoulder at them. "Mom is ripped, and we have to get her to her room before she melts into a blob of nothing."

"I object to being treated as if I'm incapable of moving," Mom protested. "I'm mildly intoxicated, not flat-out snockered. Your father is another issue. Where is he?"

"Devon insisted on taking Fang to the local, despite them hitting a few pubs earlier in the day, and Brother went along to keep an eye on them, or so he said. Iain, Corbin, Amy, and Kathie all decided to accompany them."

"A pub?" Mom asked, wobbling as she made a vague gesture. "We already had champagne. Perhaps I should call him. ..."

"It'll be fine. The others won't let him go crazy any more than they would Fang," I said in my Mom-soothing voice, which, oddly enough, was the same tone I used when trying to lure the Eltons back into their pasture. "Not that I'm worried about Fang, because he won't have more than a pint, and I can't see Brother doing anything to jeopardize his big tour and tea tomorrow."

Mom stopped halfway up the stairs to the floor with our rooms. "Emily, I have to ask. I know you said it doesn't matter, but I want you to think one last time about the wedding—"

"There's no need," I interrupted here, and with a little push got her moving upward again. "I swear to anything you like that I'm not in the least bit bothered about Brother not being at the ceremony. Now come on, let's get you poured into bed so you can be a radiant mom of the bride."

"Pour," Mom said with a snort that had her wobbling again. I clutched her arm and gave her another little push. "What? Oh. Where did that step come from? Very well. Tallyho and up we go!"

Holly and Marla, both giggling behind me, assisted in getting Mom into her jammies and comfortable in bed with a bottle of water, the small box of chocolates Mace had placed in each of the rooms, and the TV remote. When we left, she was happily chomping on the chockies while texting pictures from the hen party to my grandmother.

I closed her door, leaning against it while I looked at Holly and Marla.

"It's been a hell of a day," I said, my limbs a bit rubbery after all the pampering at the spa. "Did you notice—"

I stopped when a man emerged from around a corner that led to the back stairs. He jumped in surprise at seeing us, swallowed hard a couple of times, then dug through a pocket of his jacket and pulled out a small black box bearing a couple of electronic screens.

"Oh! Erm … hello. I'm with Spirited Lives. We're ghost seekers." He held up the box. "This is my thermal imager. It shows me spirits that you can't see with the naked eye."

"Thermal imaging?" I asked, straightening up to get a look at it. "I don't understand how that can see a spirit unless it has a mass that allows it to conduct energy. Namely, a heat signature. May I see it?"

"Erm …" The man swallowed again, and backed up a spot. "I shouldn't. It's very valuable, and Leon wouldn't like it."

"It's OK. Emily's a physicist," Holly said, giving him a supportive smile. "She is dead keen on things like thermal imaging."

"It's a little hobby," I admitted, and scooted closer so I could see just what readouts the device had.

The man made a garbled sound, then spun around and dashed off without another word. Loud footsteps thundered up the wooden back stairs. We waited until the faint thud of a door closing on the upper level drifted down, then looked at each other.

"Odd," Holly said, her expression thoughtful.

"Downright weird," I agreed. "Well, I suppose I should pick up Herbert, and go to—ack!"

Behind where Holly and Marla stood with arms entwined around waists, the face of a woman loomed up out of the darkness, making me start.

They spun around as the woman's lips stretched into a smile. "Oh, hello. I thought you had all gone to bed."

"We are," I answered slowly. It was one of the waitresses that Mace had brought on to help with the wedding-related meals. While she seemed innocuous enough, I wondered why she was wandering around the guest rooms. "Is there something we can help you with?"

"No, nothing, thank you. I'm just picking up the tray that was ordered in one of the rooms."

"Ah. Room service," I said, watching when she sidled past us and headed to the corridor that led to Devon's room. "Good night!"

"And a very pleasant evening to you ladies," she said with another lip-stretched smile that for some bizarre reason made me think of the Slender Man creepypasta.

Holly, Marla, and I faced one another. "I'm getting Herbert," I said, a profound sense of unreality claiming me.

"I think that's a good idea. Does Fang have a key to your room?" Marla asked as we proceeded down the hall to their room.

I'd left Herbert there just in case any cop arrived possessed with the knowledge that Bess was my sister, thus leaving me the likely—if unknowing—recipient of her hot birds.

"Yes. I'll lock the door." Ten minutes later, Herbert had been let out of his carrier, protesting mildly when I offered him fresh water. He graciously accepted a couple of chopped grapes, ruffled his feathers and pecked at a few that didn't fall back into place tidily, then blinked at me until I put him back into the carrier, and made a little towel nest for him.

I checked my phone, but Fang hadn't texted, and I didn't want to interrupt his guy time. "Lord knows he gets little enough free time, and then it's usually spent with me," I told Herbert. "It's good for him to let his hair down a bit and be wild and crazy."

Herbert made sleepy cooing noises before burrowing into the towel cave.

"I agree. Wild and crazy within limits." I rolled over, made a face, then swapped Fang's pillow with mine so I could bury my face into his delicious scent, and went to sleep.

The sun was out the following morning, promising a lovely day.

"Holly, have you seen Brother?" The voice drifting into the dining room from reception was my mother's. I was pleased to hear she didn't sound hungover.

"Not this morning. I can ask—there she is. Marla, have you seen Dr. Williams?"

I set down my coffee cup, and gave exactly one quarter of a smile to the fact that although Holly had no problem calling my mom Chris, she could not get over an initial impression that Brother was a highly regarded medieval scholar, and still referred to him so formally.

"I haven't, I'm afraid. Is he missing?"

The three women entered the room at that point, Holly and Marla immediately making a beeline to a table for two that sat overlooking the hyacinth bower. That table was a hot commodity within the wedding party, and everyone coveted it for both the lovely scenery and the fact that the hotel's cat frequently sunned himself on the ledge, within easy petting distance.

"No, I'm sure he caught the early train he said he was thinking of taking, since it would allow him more time to work on the day's puzzles. Emily—"

"I'm sure, Mom," I reassured her for the umpteenth time. "To be absolutely honest, it's a toss-up on whether I'd be here if Brother had been able to get me a ticket for the tour and tea. I probably would skip the ceremony if Fang went with me. Regardless, I'm happy Brother is having such a fabulous experience."

"Where's Fang?" Mom asked, having switched her concern to what delicious offerings Mace and Gerard had whipped up for breakfast. "Oh dear lord, are those orange cranberry scones? You know I have exactly zero resistance against orange cranberry scones. I cannot stop eating them!"

"That's exactly why I asked Mace to make some," I said, popping the end bit of a nearly orgasmic orange cranberry scone into my mouth, and trying not to moan with mingled hangover and appreciation of Mace's scones. "It's working miracles on my wonky brain."

"Wonky brain? Oh, a hangover?" Mom said, scoffing as she scooped up a plateful of herbed eggs, sausage, toast, and potatoes. "You hardly drank anything. Your aunt is the one who should have a hangover. She and Amy were having a good time over a few bottles of prosecco."

I looked up from where I was staring into my coffee. Gerard, Fang and I had discovered, had a near obsession with roasting his own coffee, and it made our coffee-loving hearts soar with happiness to drink the results of his extensive labor. "Uh-oh. Is that hurt feelings I hear? Did they leave you out? That's not like Kathie."

"No, no, it was nothing like that," Mom said quickly. "I'm not tattling at all. I'm simply mentioning if anyone has a hangover, it should be her and not you."

I thought of pointing out my mother was in no condition to throw stones, but the truth was, she was as bright and perky as she was normally. There wasn't even a hint of wincing when she went to stand at the window gazing out at the sun-filled garden, whereas when I had done the same thing twenty minutes before, I had careened back from the sunlight like an elderly vampire.

"Where is Fang?" Mom asked again as she sat at the table with me.

"Face down on the bed with his shirt and shoes on, and nothing else," I told her, remembering the pale-pink lipstick I'd used to put a smiley face on his bare ass. I leaned down to pop a bit of strawberry into Herbert's carrier. He cooed at it and smacked his beak quite a bit. I assumed that meant he enjoyed it, and chopped up another one.

"That is frequently the way of bachelor parties," Mom said around a mouth of eggs and sausage. "I expected Brother to be in a similar state, but evidently he got himself dressed and off without waking me up. Ah well, I'm sure he'll appreciate the video of the wedding. If you're—"

"That's it," I said, rising and picking up Herbert's carrier. "I'm putting a moratorium on questions about my feelings, which I have made perfectly clear both in writing and verbally. I shall now go to the spa in order to sweat for half an hour. That ought to get rid of any leftover booze toxins."

"Spa?" Amy and Kathie stood in the doorway, both wearing sunglasses. Their expressions were pained, and Amy had a faint green cast to her complexion, while Kathie clutched the doorframe with an air of desperation. Behind her, Clara stood with her phone in her hand, tapping away.

Kathie said, "Sweat? Are you talking about the sauna? Oh god, that sounds heavenly. I can lie there and let the heat suck out all the bad. Clara, would you like to try the sauna?"

She looked up, scrunched her nose, and then, after a moment's thought, shook her head. "I don't like to get sweaty. I'll stay here with Dad."

"You are an angel child, with your father's good looks and my smarts," Kathie said, giving her a swift ruffle of the hair before both women turned a careful about-face and, holding on to each other's arms, stumbled off toward the spa.

"I'll watch over your mom," I told Clara, who, like my mother, had her focus narrowed on the breakfast offerings.

She murmured something, but her eyes lit as she beheld the food.

"Mom, sauna after you eat?" I asked.

She waggled a hand. "Perhaps. It's an hour until makeup and hair, yes?"

"Yes, but it's not really going to be hair and make-up, per se. It's just Holly fixing my hair, and Marla doing the makeup."

"Marla is so good with makeup," Holly piped in from the coveted table. Even Clara had given them a sour look, since Dobby, the cat, was a favorite with her. "She does the best zombie you've ever seen. She manages to make it look like the veins on your neck are open and oozing—"

"Yeah, that's not going down well," I said at a small protest from my stomach. "I'm going to sweat. Join if you want; otherwise, I'll see everyone in an hour."

Iain and Corbin were midway down the stairs when I hurried away, but other than accepting their happy wishes for the day, I didn't stay to chat.

Fang, I mused. Like my aunt, I stretched out on one of the wooden benches, mentally encourag-ing my body to exude the remaining alcohol via my pores. Fang was no doubt still sleeping it off, but I was loath to wake him up. He so seldom had days when he could sleep in.

"I don't want to disturb Fang until it's time to get married," I announced to the sauna in general.

By then, it was full of my mother, Kathie, Amy, and, oddly enough, Devon, who lay on the bench opposite in a pair of extremely small white Speedos, a towel covering his face. I had an idea he was actually sleeping, but figured maybe his pores were working for him, too. "Would you mind if I got dressed in your room, Mom?"

"Our room is bigger," Marla offered. "You're all welcome to dress there."

"Sounds like a party," Mom said, and the others agreed, including Devon.

"I thought you were asleep," I told him, nudging the towel with my toe.

"I was. That, or I was briefly deceased," he answered, clutching the towel. "Stop that."

I made a face at him. "You know better than to get drunk the night before your best friend gets married."

He muttered something.

"What?" I asked.

He sighed, and said loudly, "I said, bite my ass."

I laughed, as did the others. "So very grumpy. I don't remember your previous hangovers making you this crabby before."

He pulled up the towel just enough to glare at me with one baleful eye. "Kindly stop stabbing your words into my brain, and let me die in peace."

"Fang is probably already up, has had breakfast, and is zooming around making sure everything is good," I said without a shred of confidence behind my words.

"He can bite my ass, too," came the muffled reply.

"You've got two hours to get over your hangover,"

I told him, rising and clutching my towel to myself. Amy and Kathie were chatting in the corner about books, and my mother had just exited, citing a need for a shower before she got dressed.

I followed her back to the hotel, stopping by the spa reception to pick up Herbert, who had been enjoying being spoiled by Kim, the nail tech.

I expected to find Fang still snoozing, but to my surprise, our room was barren of any sexy vets.

Instead, it was full of Bess and Monk.

In Ren Faire costumes.

"Oh, hello," I said, pausing to note my sister's pale-blue Arwen dress (complete with silver-leaf accessories) and her husband's Aragorn ensemble. He also bore a sword strapped to his waist. "What are you guys doing in my room? I told you we had one for you. It's to the right, left at the T. It's opposite the back stairs."

"We can't stay, not beyond your wedding," Bess said, glancing around the room. "Where did you put Herbert?"

"He's safe," I said, having stashed him with Amy's husband, Corbin, who evidently had a fondness for birds. "We're about to do hair and makeup, such as it is. Er … that's a nice dress. Is Monk being Viggo?"

"Of course," she said, brushing her hand down her gown. "Is there anyone else?"

"We are a family of Viggo fans," I admitted. "Did you want to do the getting-ready thing with us? Kathie will be there, as well as Holly and Marla, and Amy, a new friend who runs a gaming company with her husband."

"No, I won't, if it's no matter to you," Bess said, examining herself in the mirror, touching an intricately braided hairstyle, which was dotted with more silver leaf. I had no doubt she knew how well she looked. She definitely favored our blond mother more, while I had to live with hair that was turning into Brother's shade of brown with each year that passed. "But if you'd like me there, I can send Monk into hiding until we're sure the coast is clear."

"Huh?" I asked, gathering up a cosmetic bag into which I'd stuffed everything I would need to be made presentable. "Why does he have to hide? You can't possibly expect bird-fighting villains to crash my party."

"You don't know them like we do," Monk said, sitting on the foot of the bed, and turning on the TV.

I had to give him that point. "Why don't you go to your own room," I said, shooing them toward the door. "You can't stay here, because at some point, Fang will come back to change."

"We can't," Bess said, spinning around to examine her backside. "There are people hanging around the corridor."

"People? People not our family? Was it Amy and Corbin?" I briefly described them.

"No. Some dude with lizards on his pants was hovering at the landing, and he hid around the corner when Monk tried to go into our room." She carefully seated herself at the small table and helped herself to our "Wedding Morning Noms So You Don't Faint Walking down the Aisle" spread that Mace had delivered earlier. I noticed that Fang had eaten the croissants and fruit I'd left him, so at least he wasn't suffering the same hangover that affected Devon. "This looks good. Is it vegan?"

"It's goat's cheese, so I'm going to say no," I answered, typing a text to Fang. We'd made a promise that once we had separated for morning activities, we wouldn't see each other again until the ceremony. I thought it was a bit silly, but Fang was all for it.

"Eh. It's good I'm not vegan yet," Bess said, and stuffed a cracker with rosemary lemon feta into her mouth. "What's up? You missing your fiancé?"

"Just checking where he is. Ah. He's off at the local shop buying Devon some pain meds, and a package of bandages because his new shoes rubbed a blister last night."

"That's it?" Bess said, spreading one of the cloth napkins that we hadn't used, and loading up a small plate. She stopped to shoot me a questioning look. "Where's the romance? Where's the sense of expectant anticipation? Where's your air of delicate maidenhood about to flower? Get with it, Emily! It's your wedding day."

"One in which I'm destined to go hungry if you keep eating my special-day shit," I said, moving just out of her reach a little bit of smoked salmon that I'd left alone because I didn't want to have salmon breath when I went in for the official kiss.

"*Special-day shit?* This is exactly what I'm talking about," Bess said, stuffing more bread and cheese in around her words. "I swear, you don't have a romantic bone in your body. Poor Fang. Do you even tell him you love him?"

"Of course I do, and don't be so judgmental," I said perilously close to a snap. That she was being snarky with me I tolerated, because I didn't really care what she thought about my life, but when she started talking trash about Fang, the situation was different. "You wanted a big-ass, flower-laden ceremony at a temple in Spain with three hundred people, and you had that. Fang and I aren't interested in anything beyond what we've arranged for—namely, the chance to see everyone, get the legal stuff over with, and then go on our happy way. Now, please go to your own room so Fang won't feel weird when he changes."

"There's someone—" Bess started to say.

"I'll go check and make sure the coast is clear, all right?" I stopped myself from muttering as I went to check the various hallways, but it was a near thing. "There's no one."

Bess opened my door a crack, one eyeball squinting at me.

I made shooing motions. "Go to your room that Fang and I are paying for, please. I want to let people make my hair look under control, for a change."

"Fine, but don't blame us if we end up in jail again because you couldn't let us hang in your room," my sister said, snatching up a plate of lemon and raspberry macarons that I was planning on saving for an after-ceremony pick-me-up. "Just think of how many birds like Herbert will suffer if we go to jail!"

I said nothing, but waited for her and Monk to lock their door before I returned to grab my dress, sandals, and cosmetics.

EIGHT
THE DENOUEMENT
CROWS AT MIDNIGHT

EMILY
August 18ᵗʰ

"Dear friends—old and new—and beloved family members, you are welcome here to witness the exchange of rings and promises by Fang and Emily." The officiant, a friend of Holly's, entered the garden and stood before us in a white pantsuit and with what I could only think of as a lei of white flowers. She beamed first at everyone, then focused on us, her smile growing until she noticed the pillow that Holly (maid of honor) held. "Er …"

"His name is Herbert," I said, carefully adjusting the cowboy suit that Holly thought was his way of dressing up. "Yes, he's a pigeon, a former fighter, but now retired. If you're worried about the outfit, you needn't be. Fang looked him over a little bit ago, and said that not only does Herbert appear in good shape" considering his background, but also the costume doesn't rub or hurt him."

"Erm …" the officiant said, still looking at Herbert, who sat on the pillow next to the rings. He looked quite interested in the proceedings.

"He is a former fighter and will now be living a life of ease and comfort," I reassured the officiant. No doubt she was concerned about his welfare.

"The location of where he will do so is yet to be decided," Fang chimed in, giving me a raised eyebrow that said much.

"You're lucky I speak your eyebrow language," I told him. We hadn't had long to discuss what to do with Herbert, but I wasn't going to miss the opportunity to have a pigeon in a cowboy costume be ring bearer at my wedding, even if I didn't get to add him to our menagerie.

"I am *very* lucky," he said, squeezing my hands, and giving me a look so scorching, I almost pulled one of my hands from his to fan myself.

Almost.

"Yes, well, such as that is, we have a joyous journey to share with Emily and Fang. I'd like to invite the bride and groom to read their statements." She gave Fang a little nod to begin.

"Statements?" I heard Bess asking from behind me. "Shouldn't it be vows?"

"We're nontraditional," I reminded her.

"You are *so* weird," she told me. "I mean, look at your dress!"

I looked down at myself. Fang and I had decided that if we were going to spend a lot of money on a suit and a dress, we wanted maximum use from them. He got a lovely suit of forest green so dark, it was almost black, while I went for a dark-green cocktail dress made heavy with detailed silver beads, with a wonderfully dramatic scalloped high-low mermaid hem.

I wanted to point out that she was well beyond weird, but figured this was the time to keep that sort of thought to myself. "My dress is gorgeous, and can be worn at any fancy event."

"It's not bridal," Bess muttered, but everyone ignored her.

"So long as you and Fang are happy, that's what's important," Mom intervened, and gestured to go on.

"Can I say again just how much I like your mother?" Fang said softly. "Best mother-in-law in the world."

"When she's not obsessed with her latest hobby, absolutely," I whispered back.

He cleared his throat and, holding one of my hands, said, "Emily, the day you swept into my life and changed everything was the moment my life truly began. You are my sun and stars, my moon and planets, and the poetry in my soul. And since I know this will speak to you, you will please take the equation $2(2X - i) > 4X - 6U$ and solve for i."

I blinked a couple of times, then beamed at Fang. "You sweet talker, you!"

"What on earth is that supposed to mean?" Kathie asked Iain.

"You have me there," he answered. "Is it something the younger generation says?"

"No," Clara said from where she stood next to Holly. I'd told her to pick out whatever outfit she'd like to wear, and she chose a flared sundress with giant poppies. Holly and Marla were in matching garnet suits that made me envious.

"It's an equation," I explained to everyone. They all looked confused as hell. "Fang knows how to get to a girl."

"What does it mean?" Holly asked.

"The equation solves to $i < 3\ U$." Everyone continued to stare, their expressions going comical. "I heart you? The greater sign and number 3 make a heart … never mind. I'll write it all out for you guys later," I told them.

"Emily, would you like to read your statement to Fang?" the officiant asked, looking a bit stunned about the eyes.

"I would, indeed," I said, giving Fang the smile I kept for him alone. I glanced at the small card that Holly extracted from my bouquet of carnations.

"Emily," Fang said in his best mock-serious voice. "Did you make an exam cheat sheet for your statement?"

"Old habits die hard," I told him, retaking his hands. "Fang, the best of all men, and the handsomest vet in the British Isles, you have always been here for me, no matter how much life decided to crap on me."

"Emily!" my mother protested gently.

Kathie, Iain, Amy, and Corbin all stifled laughter. Bess rolled her eyes and murmured something to Monk.

Holly hiccuped, but managed to keep from laughing, as she obviously wanted.

"You charmed me with your sense of humor, you spun my thoughts until they were so entangled with yours that they will never be separated, but most of all, you make me so happy that every day I get up and want to dance and sing and do things to you that wouldn't be at all appropriate to mention here, but you can bet your bottom dollar that tonight, I'm going to tell you just exactly what I want to do."

Fang burst out laughing at that point, no doubt due to the sultry look I gave him. He squeezed my fingers before raising them to kiss them as I turned to the officiant and gave her a nod to let her know I was done.

"Since Emily and Fang have decided to forgo further vows, they will now give and receive rings that symbolize the endless circle of their love, both for each other and for those who matter to them. Can the … er … ring bearer come forward."

Holly and Herbert appeared between us, the latter looking sleepy, no doubt due to all the food I'd given him before the ceremony started.

Fang slid my ring on the appropriate finger, and leaned forward to say, "Only you would have a cowboy pigeon at our wedding. I love you so much I may explode."

"That's just the leftover hangover," I told him before placing the ring on his finger, adding, "Also, I love you beyond exploding capacity, and into the realm of the event horizon of a particularly massive black hole."

"God. Scientists," Bess said to Corbin, who just gave her a long look in return.

"By the authority bestowed upon me, I am delighted to pronounce Fang and Emily a wedded couple. Please feel free to share your first kiss as husband and—"

It was at that moment that three complete and utter strangers burst out to the garden, two women and a man.

"Here you are!" the man shouted, striking a dramatic pose and pointing at Bess. "You're not going to escape again! Santana, grab them! Rosie, find Herbert!"

"Run!" Bess shrieked, and, without so much as a blink, bolted out of the garden, Monk directly on her heels. A woman in green—clearly Santana—ran after Bess, only narrowly missing mowing down Fang in the process.

"What? Who—" I started to ask, but the man strode forward and started shouting.

"I want my property back," he bellowed as he stormed down the aisle. "And if I don't get it, I'll make sure each and every one of your damned group ends up behind bars, where you all deserve to rot."

"This is a private wedding," Iain said, his voice going very Scottish as Devon moved from Fang's side to join him in facing the intruder. "Why don't ye be movin' on until after the ceremony. Then, if you want a word with—"

"Aha! Thought you could hide him?" The woman attacker (Rosie, evidently) spotted Holly and Herbert, and started around the outside of the chair arrangement.

"Marla, protect them!" I shouted, pointing at Holly.

Marla—who was proficient in three different martial arts—stopped watching the argument and caught sight of Rosie on her way toward them. Her eyes lit with pleasure, enough so that the woman paused, obviously hesitating when faced with Marla in a defender's stance.

Rosie glanced back at her cohort in crime.

"I've had it up to here with you terrorists!" the man shouted, waving his arms around like he was a deranged windmill. "And this is the last straw, do you hear me? The *very* last straw! First you harass me in court, then you make sure the studio in Birmingham is closed down, and then you destroy my business by stealing the last of my birds. Well, no more! Leander West is a victim no more! I'll see to it that all of you are destroyed, instead!"

"You're leaving. *Now*," Devon said, and grabbed him by his sleeve.

The man Leander took objection to that, and threw a punch. It was wild, and Devon was no stranger to scrapping (as he and Fang referred to it), so he easily avoided the blow.

"Oh lord," I said, resisting when Fang pulled me behind him, though my heart warmed at the protective gesture. Could any man be more wonderful? I sniffled a happy tear and kissed the back of his neck before moving to his side, saying, "Bonus points for protective mode. Look, buster, I don't know who you are, or why you think it's OK to come to my wedding and make a scene, but—"

Fang said, "Stay here, Em," at the same time Leander shoved Devon, who, of course, shoved him back, hard enough that former stumbled backward into Iain.

"Oh!" Kathie yelled, jumping onto the seat of the wooden chair she'd been sitting on. "Don't you dare hurt Iain's owie knee! We still have to work out the details of the trail riding and yurts before he can stop farming!"

Clara pulled out her phone and started filming the chaos. "And my classes. Don't forget about my classes on making goat's milk soap."

"Good idea to film. Make sure you keep it on these crackpots," I told her, giving Rosie a glare. She was still at the far end of the chairs, Marla standing guard in front of Holly and Herbert, her gaze wavering from Leander to the men, then to Marla. "Focus on that one. We'll want video evidence of her crime."

"I'm filming, too," Amy said, and pulled out her phone.

"Should I help, do you think?" Corbin asked, glancing behind them where the man was raging. "I don't like to presume in a country that isn't my own, but on the other hand, I don't like bullies."

"Let's hold back and jump in if we're needed," Amy told him, and they rose, blocking off the side aisle as they both had their phones out, filming the fracas.

The shoving match had Fang moving forward; he clearly intended on helping get rid of the evil Leander. Unfortunately, at that moment, the man in question threw another punch at Devon.

Devon, sensing movement behind him, both dodged the blow and turned while stepping back. Fang, suddenly in range, took the stranger's fist straight to his nose. He shouted something in Welsh and threw himself on the man, both of them going down into a heap of legs and arms and the carnations from one of the buckets of flowers that bedecked the end of the aisle.

"Careful, he's got a knife!" Devon shouted, dancing around as Fang and the man rolled around, fists still flying.

Mom, who had moved over to stand with Holly and Marla, gasped.

"Stay with her," Marla told Mom, and vaulted the two rows of seats to join the fray.

"Get the knife!" I yelled, and hoisted up the hem of my dress in preparation to running forward to defend my fallen hero, but at that moment, Rosie leaped forward, knocking down a chair as she did so.

"Not today, Satan!" I bellowed as I caught sight of her heading for Herbert. I threw myself sideways, grabbing Rosie as she lunged toward Mom and Holly. I caught only an edge of her shirt, however, and ended up face down on the grass. I was stunned for a few seconds, but managed to lift up my head, spit out a bit of grass, and yell, "Mom! Protect Herbert!"

"Come on, my dashing Earless Erica! There're innocent people to save!" Corbin said as he and Amy hurried down the side, moving up behind the woman. My mother, who once did a six-month course on personal protection, calmly pulled out a (no-doubt highly illegal in England) bottle of pepper spray and showed it to Rosie. "I will spray you if you take one more step forward," Mom threatened. "This is gel, so where it lands, it stays. Trust me, you don't want pepper gel staying in your eyes."

The woman stumbled to stop just as Amy and Corbin grabbed her by either arm.

"A knife? Don't you dare touch him!" My aunt's voice rose above the general sounds of fighting from Fang, Leander, and now Devon, who had somehow been absorbed into the tangle of flailing men.

Kathie was clearly already fired up by the attack on her husband, and took offense.

"That's my new nephew-in-law, and he's a vet. Do you know how valuable it is to have a vet in the family? He's worth his weight in gold!" she shouted from atop a chair, and tried to jump on Leander's back when he managed to get to his feet, but Iain caught her in midleap and swung her around to safety.

"Cool," I heard Clara say. She grinned when Kathie grabbed Iain's hair and pulled his head down for what appeared to be a hell of a kiss.

"That's a rather nepotistic attitude," I heard Corbin tell Amy in a whisper. "Fang is worth more than just his profession."

"You're not a pet owner," I told him, having caught my breath enough to get to my feet before yelling my reassurance to Fang that I was fine. Iain and Devon were holding the bastard Leander back, while Fang lurched to the side to sit down hard on a chair.

"We are, actually. We have three dogs, but I admit that Amy is the one who usually deals with vet visits," Corbin said with a sheepish expression.

"He's extremely squeamish when it comes to the dogs," Amy told me. "People can be splattered all over the place and he won't turn a hair, but a blood draw at the vet has him hyperventilating. He's too empathetic."

"Mm-hmm," I said, withholding judgment, although I couldn't help but feel a bit smug about Fang. He really was the most perfect man. I rose and turned, intending on telling him that when a scream from behind me had me spinning around.

Santana, who'd gone after Bess and Monk, now rushed into the garden. Rosie used that as a diversion, allowing her to escape Amy and Corbin's hold.

Santana tried to jump on Holly as Rosie shoved Mom aside, sending her tumbling into a thankfully not too dense shrub, before swinging at the nearest person, who happened to be Amy. That resulted in Corbin shouting and rushing her, while Amy danced backward, her phone in her hands as she filmed.

"Mom, are you—"

"I'm fine," she said. The only thing visible of her was her legs and one hand that waggled wildly. "Get the bird!"

"You are the best mom," I told her, and spun around to help Holly.

To my horror, Santana had pounced on Holly and was trying to wrestle Herbert from her hold. The words that came out of my mouth had the volume of a randy bull yelling for female companionship. "Don't you touch a dear little feather on that pigeon's head! Holly is a former nun and will defend him with her life!"

Holly shot me a quick startled glance before wrenching back the pillow bearing the now-awake and slightly squawking Herbert.

"I don't care who she is—I just want our birds back, and your group of terrorists in prison!" Santana said in a snarl, and lunged again at Holly, who leaped backward directly into a planter.

She shrieked as she tipped to the side, almost falling. Marla, hearing Holly, abandoned trying to help Devon tie up Leander, and vaulted over the chairs that stood between us, screaming, "No one touches my wife!"

Before I could do more than take Herbert from Holly, Marla grabbed the woman threatening us, and flipped her with so much force she bounced into a bed of some sort of fuzzy blue flower. Evidently it was planted there for bees, because the second the woman hit the (relatively) soft flower bed, she scrambled away with her left side covered in bright-yellow pollen. "What is—ack! Pollen! I'm allergic! GET IT OFF ME!" she yelled as she slapped at all the pollen blotches on her black pants before running into the dining area, where I could see her dunking napkins in a water pitcher and wiping off her clothes.

Mom emerged from the shrub looking a bit leafy, but no worse for wear.

"Here, take him. Guard him with your life," I said, shoving Herbert at her before turning to face Fang. "We should call the police. These people are bad—hey!"

Rosie had been arguing with Devon, Iain, and Kathie, but when she saw Mom holding Herbert, she headed straight for her.

I leaped in front of Mom and spread my arms. "No one hurts my mother, my friend, or sweet little Herbert."

To my utter surprise, the woman halted, giving me a puzzled look. "Hurt him? Why would I hurt him? I want to save him from you terrorists."

"No one here is a terrorist," I said firmly, continuing to stand in front of my mother, although I did lower my arms. "This is my wedding, and I'll thank you to back the fuck off and let us party in peace."

"Emily," Mom said in the mildly disapproving voice she keeps for the f-bomb. Not that she didn't drop one on occasion, but she preferred to pretend she didn't.

"You seem to think you are the main character here," Rosie argued. She stood with her hands on her hips, now looking annoyed more than angry. "You are not. I am. Or rather, *we* are. You stole our birds for some heinous purpose—"

"Oh, I like that," I interrupted, waving a hand to emphasize my disbelief. Evidently, it caught Fang's attention, because he lurched up and staggered down the aisle to me. "You call us heinous? *You're* the evil one! People like you who indulge in something so completely reprehensible and inhuman as bird fighting are not main characters—they're villains, and they get what they deserve. Oh, Fang, no! Not both eyes!"

The woman did a double take when Fang stopped next to me, blood seeping from his nose, while both eyes had dark rings that were growing darker with each passing moment.

"Is it bad? Iain set my nose," he answered, wincing as he touched his nose. "Why are you doing this?"

"You people are trying to harm our birds, that's why we are here. Leander! I'm done trying to reason with them. I'm calling the police," Rosie yelled.

"You can't call the cops—*we* are calling the cops," Kathie snapped back. Iain and Devon had Leander sitting on a chair, his head drooping as he leaned forward, clearly feeling the effect of tangling with Devon and Fang.

Fang asked me, "Why does she think we're doing something wrong?"

"I don't know," I answered slowly, my eyes on the woman as she turned away to explain to someone on the phone that she was reporting an assault and needed police intervention. "But I suspect something is going on other than what Bess told us."

I could tell Fang was going to roll his eyes, but at the movement, he winced.

"Just so you know," I said loudly to Rosie as she continued to speak on the phone, "I will be informing the police about your bird-fighting ring."

"Bird fighting? We don't teach our birds to fight," she said, turning to nod at Herbert. "His gun isn't real. I mean, how could it be? It's tiny. But regardless, we never have fighting. Our videos are all suitable for children."

I stared at her for a moment, then met Fang's gaze. "They aren't a bird-fighting ring," he told me.

"Bess was wrong," I agreed, then asked the woman, "We were told you made the birds fight each other. What do you do with them if not that?"

"We would never!" she said, outraged, gesturing toward Herbert. "We love our birdies! We are Dinosaurs with Feathers."

She said that like we should know the name.

"Eh … " I said.

"For heaven's sakes … we make the videos where our birds live in a virtual town called Kneecap Hollow. We film them going about their day."

Fang and I stared blankly at her.

She slapped her thighs. "We've won awards in the short-video category! You must have heard of us!"

"Sorry, we haven't, but I'm relieved to know you aren't being heinous to the birds." I glanced at where Mom was absently feeding Herbert some veggies from the buffet. "I suppose you should take him home, although my brand-new husband is a vet, so—"

"No," Fang said, pulling me up for a fast kiss. "He had a home that isn't abusing him. We don't need to take him to the States with us."

"So, are we letting this bastard up, or what?" Kathie called from the other end of the aisle, gesturing toward Leander with a small pocketknife that I assumed had been wrestled from him.

"Yes, let him go, although I think he needs to see some consequences for coming in here with a knife and attacking everyone," I said, after I murmured to Mom that she could let the woman have Herbert.

Santana emerged from the dining room, sneezing and looking annoyed as she stood and glared at Marla.

"It's wrong to be happy. I'm going to hell in a handbasket," I told Fang softly.

He followed my gaze, and chuckled. "Normally, I would argue for more tolerance, but she all but attacked Holly. Assuming her allergies aren't severe, I'm sure she'll survive, hopefully in possession of a little more common sense."

We started up the aisle, intending on explaining the miscommunication between the bird people and us, but before we made it two steps, a commotion started inside the hotel and burst out into the garden.

Two of the ghost hunters leaped across the chairs, heading for the far entrance, but before they made it, four policemen in blue flak jackets appeared.

The ghost hunters stopped dead, and I think might have made a run for the brick fence, but the hotel's servers boiled out to join us.

Bringing with them a very red-faced, pajama-wearing Brother.

NINE
A BRAVE NEW FUTURE

KATHIE
18 August

"What on earth is all this? Fang, dear, don't leave, you and Emily have to finish the wedding." Chris hurried over to where Brother was stabbing the air with a forefinger as he loudly insisted someone be arrested. "Brother, what are you doing here? You should be at the Sherlock Holmes house."

"I know I should," he answered, pausing in mid–air stab to glare at her. "I was kidnapped! And now my entire day is ruined. No, not day … year! Chief Inspector Mortimer will be demoted after this, I just know it. And I've worked so hard to get through the Murder of the Barking Ewe at Midnight. Dammit!"

"Kidnapped?" Fang and Emily asked at the same time.

"By who?" I asked, catching sight of a very pale innkeeper peeking out of a half-opened door. "And I second Chris's question—what's going on?"

Iain, being the brilliant man he is, immediately went to speak with one of the uniformed police. I watched a bit worriedly as his eyebrows rose every few seconds.

Clara filmed him for half a minute before turning her attention to the intruders. The uniformed cops had made a quick job of restraining the two ghost hunters, who now sat on the grass with hands zip-tied behind their respective backs, while bearing disgruntled expressions. Although it struck me that the man with the turtle pants looked somewhat pleased at the same time.

I intercepted Iain as Emily, Fang, and Chris descended upon Brother. Corbin and Amy—both of whom we had taken a liking to, having spent a few hours in a pub with them the previous night—moved in to talk.

"Surely this sort of thing isn't normal here," Corbin asked. "Kidnapping tourists would appear to indicate a more extreme society than BritBox led us to believe."

"Oh, we're very cool here, normally," I said, glancing at Iain when he put one arm around me, and the other around Clara. "Football matches aside. What did the cop have to say, Iain?"

"It would appear there's been a right muck up going on under our noses," he started to say, but before he could get further, the bossy server clapped her hands and said loudly, "We will need to take statements from all of you. If you will make your way to the dining room in an orderly fashion, we'll take you in turn."

"Huh?" Amy asked, looking as confused as I felt.

"She's CID," Iain said, as the woman started shooing everyone inside. "According to the local coppers, she's been working some underground burglary ring."

"Burglary!" I said, touching the ruby necklace that Iain had given me for our last anniversary. I was glad I'd worn it the whole time we'd been at the hotel.

"Emily!" Chris shouted, stopping her as she was about to go inside with the others.

"What?" Em asked.

"You didn't kiss him," she interrupted, gesturing at Fang. "You have to kiss to make the marriage legal."

I thought of explaining to her that signing the marriage documents was what made it legal, but decided Emily could do the honor.

Emily rolled her eyes, but leaned forward and gave Fang a quick peck before taking his hand and hauling him into the dining room. "There, now we're married. Brother, wait for me! I want to hear about the kidnapping."

"It's ruined my life," Brother repeated, sinking down into a chair at the largest table. He clutched his head in his hands, obviously beyond miserable. I felt badly for him, and looked to Iain in case he had any bright ideas. He frowned for a moment, then pulled out his phone.

"I am Superintendent Tole, and we have been conducting surveillance on this gang for some time. Far too long, considering how inept and disorganized they appear to be, but there you are. Our hands are tied by the current political climate."

We all stared at the woman. She must have noticed the look of appalled horror on our respective faces, because she cleared her throat, and continued in a clipped tone. "We got word they were in the area and using a local hotel for their base. I cannot say more other than your possessions were never at risk. There was a CID officer in the hotel at all times to ensure your safety."

"And yet Brother was kidnapped under their noses," Chris said under her breath. "In a hotel full of people and cops. Ironic, that."

The superintendent stiffened, but didn't so much as glance our way.

"Constable Harris will now take your statements, and once they are done, you will be free to continue your event," she said before turning to march out of the room.

"Tell them to talk to your brother first," Iain told me quietly, still tapping on his phone.

"Oh?" I asked.

He flashed a grin that melted my heart just as it always did, and for a moment, I was overwhelmed by the fact that I had such a wonderful family. "Aye, I think I'm about to become his favorite person ever."

"You think he can make his shindig?"

"If we get him out of here in the next five minutes, and I ignore most of the laws regarding speeding, yes."

I pinched his adorable behind, and went to inform Brother about Iain's suggestion. "You need to pull yourself together," I told him. It was a big sister's prerogative.

"I am perfectly pulled together," he said with much dignity, attempting to smooth his dusty and cobwebbed pajama top. "I'm also furious that if I had to miss the Conan Doyle house visit and tea, I would have been happy to watch the wedding, but because of those blaggards, I couldn't even see my youngest daughter married."

"Meh," Emily called from where she was gathered with her friends. "You know that no one but Mom cares about that."

"And even I have grown used to the idea that no one gives a fig. Not that it matters now, since you are both married properly," Chris said, beaming at Emily and Fang. "But what I don't understand is why the ghost hunters took Brother. Did they think he was a spirit? And what were they stealing?"

It took a bit before things were explained.

"You look happy," I told Iain suspiciously. "What did you find on your phone? Some way to get Brother to his shindig?"

"Yes. I'll go tell him, but not before I take the time to appreciate the fact that you married me," he said, pulling me up for a short, hard kiss before releasing me. "I'm damned lucky Clara takes after you. I'll tell your brother my idea."

Clara and I both looked after him as he moved over to squat next to where Brother was sitting, the two of them with their heads together as Iain showed him his phone.

Clara's gaze turned to me, speculation rife in it.

"No, you don't take after me," I told her with no little sense of amusement. "You're a chip straight off your dad, just like I wasn't the one to grow you from nothing."

She looked more cheerful at that thought.

"Yes!" Brother leaped to his feet and pumped the air, then rushed over to grab Emily by the shoulders, giving her a swift kiss on both cheeks, before releasing her to pump Fang's hand a couple of times, and ending with a quick hug that evidently Fang wasn't expecting. "There's a train leaving in twelve minutes that will get me to the house in time for the tea. I'll dress in the car and record my statement later."

Iain waggled his eyebrows in promise of much; then he was off to drive Brother to the train station before Superintendent Tole noticed the latter was missing.

"Well, thank god for that," Chris said, slumping down into her chair, and accepting a glass of champagne. "He had been looking forward to that tea so much. How thoughtful of Iain to offer to drive him."

"Iain is good people," Emily said, holding up a glass in a toast. "He kept that bastard from stabbing Fang!"

"Amen to that," I agreed, and we all sat down for our interviews.

An hour later the police—both the uniformed constables and the plainclothes detectives—took their leave along with the three ghost hunters. They left little behind in the way of answers, but we pieced things together as much as we could with the hotel's owner.

"My dears, it was awful not being able to breathe a word about it to anyone," the owner said, patting Emily on a shoulder. We had gathered around the large table in order to eat. "She came to me—the superintendent is head of the local CID, you know—and told me that either we kept quiet about their presence in the hotel, or we'd find ourself facing the planning committee about the hot tub."

"You have a hot tub?" Amy asked. "I didn't see one."

"It's not working right now," the owner said, and continued on as he wandered around the table, topping up everyone's champagne glasses. I kept an eye on Clara's glass, which had exactly a half inch of liquid, which fortunately, she sipped at like it was the most precious of materials. "Well, you can see how it was! We couldn't risk that—no, we couldn't risk that at all. So we took them on. They said your wedding was the perfect cover."

"You had thieves here who could have rifled our things at any time?" Corbin asked. I leaned a little to the side, just enough that I could put a hand on Iain's thigh. He was speaking quietly about some sheep disease or other but, at my touch, shot me a long, speculative look.

I pointed at the look. "Your Mini Me definitely gets that expression from you."

He winked at me, and let his fingers do a little dancing down my own leg.

"No, no, of course not!" the owner said, clearly scandalized. "As if we'd be a party to such a thing! The superintendent assured us—assured us quite firmly, you know—that they would be watching at all times, and would safeguard not only your protection but that of your possessions, as well."

"I don't believe Brother would think much of that promise," Chris said, looking slightly squidgy from almost an hour's worth of imbibing a very good year of champagne.

"No, of course not," the owner said.

I leaned into Iain. "Do you know that man's name?"

"Who?" He looked around. "The manager?"

"Yes."

"Why?" Iain asked me.

"I need it for my inner narrative," I answered, then stroked his thigh again.

He sat up straighter, his voice dropping to a whisper. "Mace Abbot, and if you continue that, you risk shocking not only your brother's family, but Clara, as well, when I scoop you up and haul you upstairs to lick every inch of you."

I thought about it, I really did, but in the end I reminded myself this was neither the time nor place. Besides, we had pressing matters still to discuss.

At least life didn't look so problematic as it had a day before.

"Then, of course, Gerard double-booked the ghost hunters—burglars, that is—and it seemed as if everything was going to come to grief. Thankfully, it's all good now." Mace spread a sunny smile over the company. "And now that Mr. Williams is off to his important meeting in time, we can focus on providing you the best wedding experience. Can I get anything for anyone?"

"Answers, please," Emily said, and several others nodded.

"I could go for a round of that, as well," Amy said. "We're a bit confused as to what happened to Emily's dad."

"Iain knows," I told her. "He's got a cat-who-ate-the-cream sort of air about him, and I just bet that means that Brother talked on the way to the train station."

Iain smiled at me, and took my hand in his, his fingers rubbing over my knuckles in a way that made my belly go warm and happy. His voice went full Scottish when he said, "Ye know me so well, lass."

"Dish," I said, allowing him to see in my eyes all the wicked things I wanted to do to him when we were alone.

His lips twitched in response, but he managed to get himself under control.

"Evidently your brother went in search of a drink after we all got back from the pub," Iain said, leaning back with obvious enjoyment. I might be the author in the family, but Iain loved the opportunity to flex his oral-storytelling muscles. "It was a bit stuffy in his room, so he went to look for something to cool him down. You remember how he was telling everyone he was with the CID? The ghost hunters heard that, and believed it. He said they were wandering the hall, and when he appeared, he demanded to know what they were doing. They hit him over the head with something, and he blacked out."

"It's a brass statue of a lurcher," Mace said, popping back into the room to remove an empty chafing dish. "It sits on the upper-landing window. We bought it in the cutest little antique shop in Ireland.

It's a bit worse for wear, but Gerard says it should come back with polish."

"Ireland," Chris said with a thoughtful look. "They had early Celts, too, didn't they? Hmm."

"But what did they expect to do with Brother?" Emily asked. She was leaning hard into Fang, who really was quite the sight with two black eyes and a red, swollen nose that defied the ice Mace provided. "I don't understand their plan. What was their goal in hiding him away?"

"According to Superintendent Tole, they koshed him on the head, then tied him up and stuck him in the furthest attic, where they planned to leave him bound until they got safely out of the area," Mace said, fussing with the buffet, even though we'd pretty much decimated it the second the police left. It was clear he wanted to remain. "The superintendent decided that your wedding would provide them with the perfect time to search their lodgings, and when they found nothing, they returned here to investigate what they had been up to in our attics. Only fancy, they were responsible for hotel thefts up and down the west coast, and they were caught here in our little place!"

He was clearly thrilled by the events, and although I knew Brother wouldn't view it in the same light, in the end, things seemed to have worked out.

"And the bird people?" Holly asked, glancing around the room just as if the answers were to be found there. "I don't think I understand what it is they do with the birds, other than they are nice, and not evil."

"I looked it up," Corbin said, taking out his phone and passing it to Holly. "They are actually quite well-known in the short-film world."

"Oh my god, look at Herbster!" Emily cried, leaning over Holly to watch. "His little strut as he walks down the street to face that posse of pigeons … Fang, are you sure—"

"Very sure," he responded quickly. "You can get a rescue pigeon in the States, if you really want one."

"You're moving home?" I asked, startled by the statement. I knew something was up with Emily, but I half expected her to announce she was pregnant. Instead, it appeared they were leaving us.

Iain's hand descended on mine, giving me the comfort needed.

"Yes." She glanced at Fang, who continued, "Emily is talking to Corbin and Amy about the possibility of working for them. That would require us to live in the States, so we're looking at the logistics of a move."

"Could you be gettin' work there?" Iain asked him.

"I'll have to deal with the licensing red tape, but it's doable," he answered.

"I won't say I'm not seriously sad at losing you, but I understand you can't turn down a good job offer." I slid a look at Amy. We had a lot in common, and I was pleased to find she shared my somewhat warped sense of humor.

"We promise to take very good care of her," Amy told me, then added, "Sorry, Fang. We'll take care of both of you."

He laughed, and shook his head. "It's a full-time job taking care of Emily, and I wouldn't be pleased with anyone else trying to take over my role. But so long as she is content, then so am I."

"Spoken like a man who's happily married," Corbin told him, his arm draped along Amy's shoulders. She grinned at him and sent him a look that had him sitting up straighter, too.

"Just because we're moving doesn't mean we won't ever come back to England," Emily told us all. "Not that I want to part ways with Amy and Corbin—assuming you want me to have the job—"

"We do," Amy said quickly.

"—but even if it all works out, it doesn't mean we'll stay there forever," she finished.

"The contract is for three years," Corbin said, nodding. "Naturally, we don't want to use you up and cast you aside, especially since Holder—he's our partner—has an idea for something new and different after this project, but we won't talk about that for some time."

"It'll be OK," Emily said, sharing a look with Fang. I was warmed to my toes by the love that shone so brightly in their faces. "So long as we're together, that's all that matters. Well, and having the animals. And a cowboy pigeon. I wonder how hard it is to make those films. If we got a little knight's outfit with a fake horse, and a rescue pigeon who didn't mind dressing up—"

The laughter of everyone there drowned out Fang's faux groan of despair.

I gave Iain's hand a nudge until he took mine again, and leaned into his arm, happy to see Emily and Fang so in love, and reassured that come what may, we would find a way to stay at the farm without it injuring or maiming Iain.

Someone turned on their phone and had a play-list piped through the speakers. Iain pulled me into his side, and nibbled discreetly on my neck when no one was looking.

Life, I decided as I did a bit of nibbling of my own, was shaping up to be even better than I'd imagined a few days ago.

"Mum? Are we going home tomorrow? Because I just found a new vendor for oils, and they have frankincense. Christmas is just four months away! I need to get frankincense and myrrh soaps out by October. Oh! I could do a whole line! I could call it the crèche line! I have to see what sorts of other scents they have, especially if I need to make enough product to fill a gift shop at home …" My child, her face filled with animation, hurried off with her phone.

Iain sighed the sigh of the deeply martyred.

"Are you going to hate it?" I whispered into his ear.

He knew what I was asking, and gave it obvious consideration.

"No," he finally answered, and I was pleased to see that the lines of strain about his mouth were less pronounced. "It makes sense. I don't know that I agree with yurts as the perfect camping solution, but I looked up some of those camping experiences, and it's well within our means. We could even put a few closer to the barn and run out a line so they'd have power."

I was silent for a moment. I knew Iain, and he loved being a sheep farmer more than anything other than our family. "And the sheep?"

He slid me a look out of the corners of his eyes. "If I told you I was wanting to keep them all?"

"Then that's what we'll do," I said without a second of hesitation, although I was mentally working through my list of people we could hire to help Iain and Mark.

"And this is why you are the only woman in the world for me," he said, giving me a kiss despite everyone moving around the room, some folks dancing, the others standing in clumps chatting. "You understand sheep."

I didn't, but you're crazy if you think I pointed that out.

"As it happens, I could let David pick through the ewes and take what he wants," Iain said, rubbing his chin as he did when he was thinking through a problem. "We can focus on a small breeding flock, small enough they could stay on the lower pastures. David'll no doubt want to lease the rest of the land for his sheep."

"I'm sure he'd be thrilled with that," I murmured, relieved at a way to keep Iain off the damned mountain.

"Aye," he agreed, his arm tightening around me. "It was a good idea you ladies came up with. It'll suit us both, and Clara will make a fortune, so she's sorted."

I laughed, and pulled him into another slow dance, this time alongside Fang and Emily, and Holly and Marla. "Come along, you sexy Highlander, you. I think your knee can probably handle this."

"It can handle a little dancing, and a lot more later," he said sotto voce, his eyebrows waggling in a way that had me laughing with the sheer joy of the moment.

Emily and Fang's future was confirmed if Amy's confidences were accurate, and we'd continue on with a brave new future.

"You know," I told him as he pulled my hips tight against him, "this is going to sound strange … I wonder if they have a pigeon rescue around us. After seeing Emily's cute pigeon, we could have a couple for the tourists to admire. I won't go so far as to dress them up in costumes, but we could totally have a small herd of pigeons play with toys and things. The tourists would eat that up. I think maybe four pigeons. That sounds doable."

Iain's shout of laughter startled everyone but me.

EMILY'S FAM AND FRIENDS GROUP CHAT

ME

We're leaving, on a jet plane … Well, we will be in two months.

DRU

You accepted the job? You're going to move back home? Huzzah!

ME

Yup to both, although since we have to be close to an airport, yet somewhat rural, we are looking in Oregon for houses with a few acres, because you know how Fang attracts animals.

FANG

Ahem. I am not the one who brings home every single one of our pets.

ME

You suck them in with your fabulousness. Then I see them, and it's all over. So really, it's all your fault.

DRU

I'd laugh, but since we now have two girl bearded lizards named Thelma and Louise added to the menagerie, I have no grounds for it. Besides, we're doing good by giving animals loving homes.

ME

See? It's not my fault. Regardless, attached is a couple of photos from our wedding for your viewing enjoyment.

DRU

Um … why does Fang have two black eyes? Is that a leafy branch poking out of your mom's hair? Is there a reason a pigeon is standing on your head? Is it real or stuffed? It's not some sort of weird tiara, is it? Did Bess give it to you? Why did you decide to wear a stuffed cowboy pigeon tiara?

BROTHER

It's Emily's wedding. I believe, given your knowledge of her, that is sufficient explanation for all of the above.

DRU

Point taken.

BROTHER

Chief Detective Inspector Mortimer out!